FEB 1 5

THE ZOO BOX

ARIEL COHN ★ ARON NELS STEINKE

First Second
New York

FOR MARLEN

First Second

Text copyright © 2014 by Ariel Cohn
Art copyright © 2014 by Aron Nels Steinke
Compilation copyright © 2014 by Ariel Cohn and Aron Nels Steinke

Published by First Second
First Second is an imprint of Roaring Brook Press, a division of Holtzbrinck Publishing Holdings Limited Partnership
175 Fifth Avenue, New York, New York 10010

Cataloging-in-Publication Data is on file at the Library of Congress.

ISBN 978-1-62672-052-7

First Second books may be purchased for business or promotional use. For information on bulk purchases please contact Macmillan Corporate and Premium Sales Department at (800) 221-7945 x5442 or by email at specialmarkets@macmillan.com.

First edition 2014
Book design by Colleen AF Venable

Printed in China by Toppan Leefung Printing Co. Ltd., Dongguan City, Guangdong Province

1 3 5 7 9 10 8 6 4 2

BY ART WE LIVE

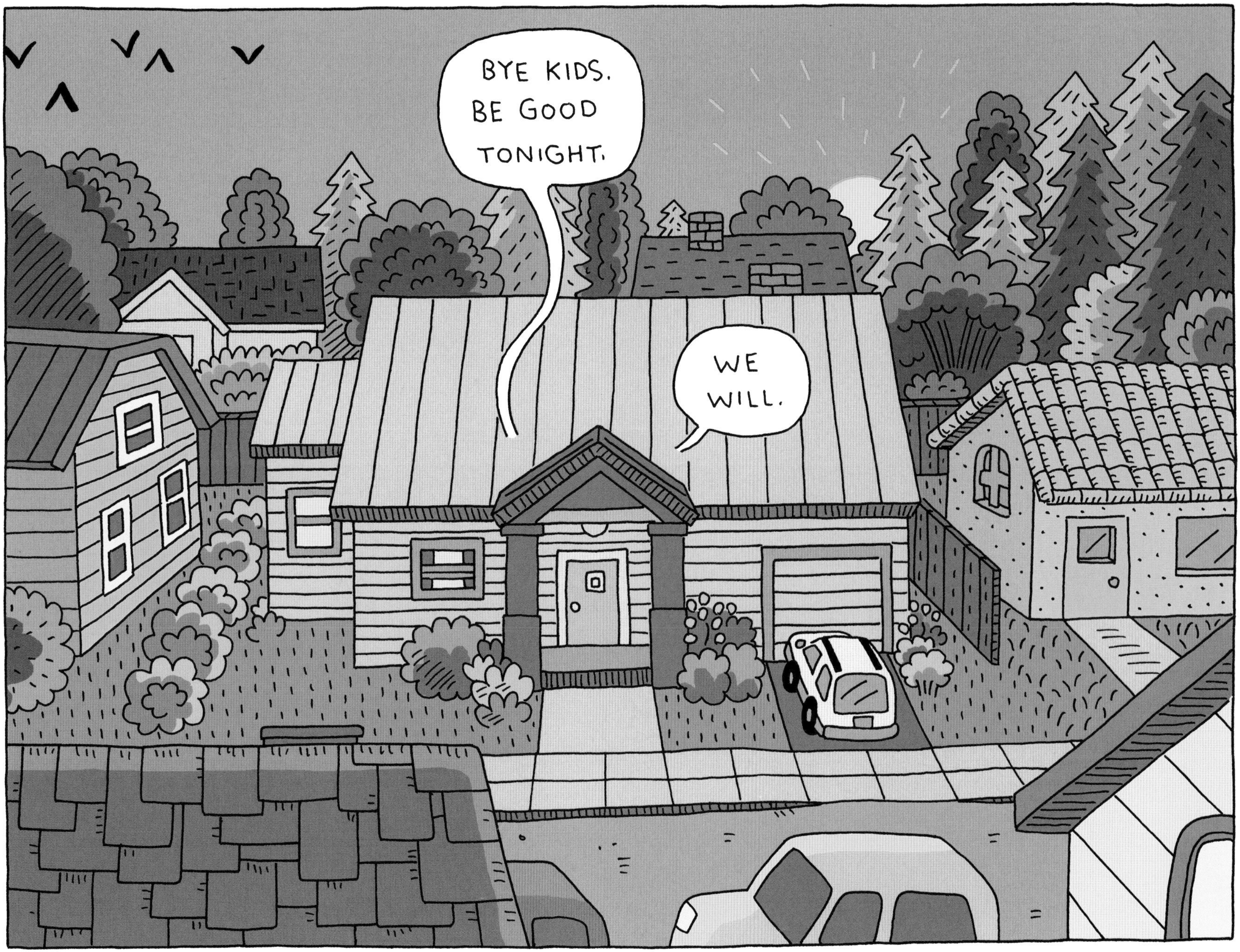
BYE KIDS. BE GOOD TONIGHT.
WE WILL.

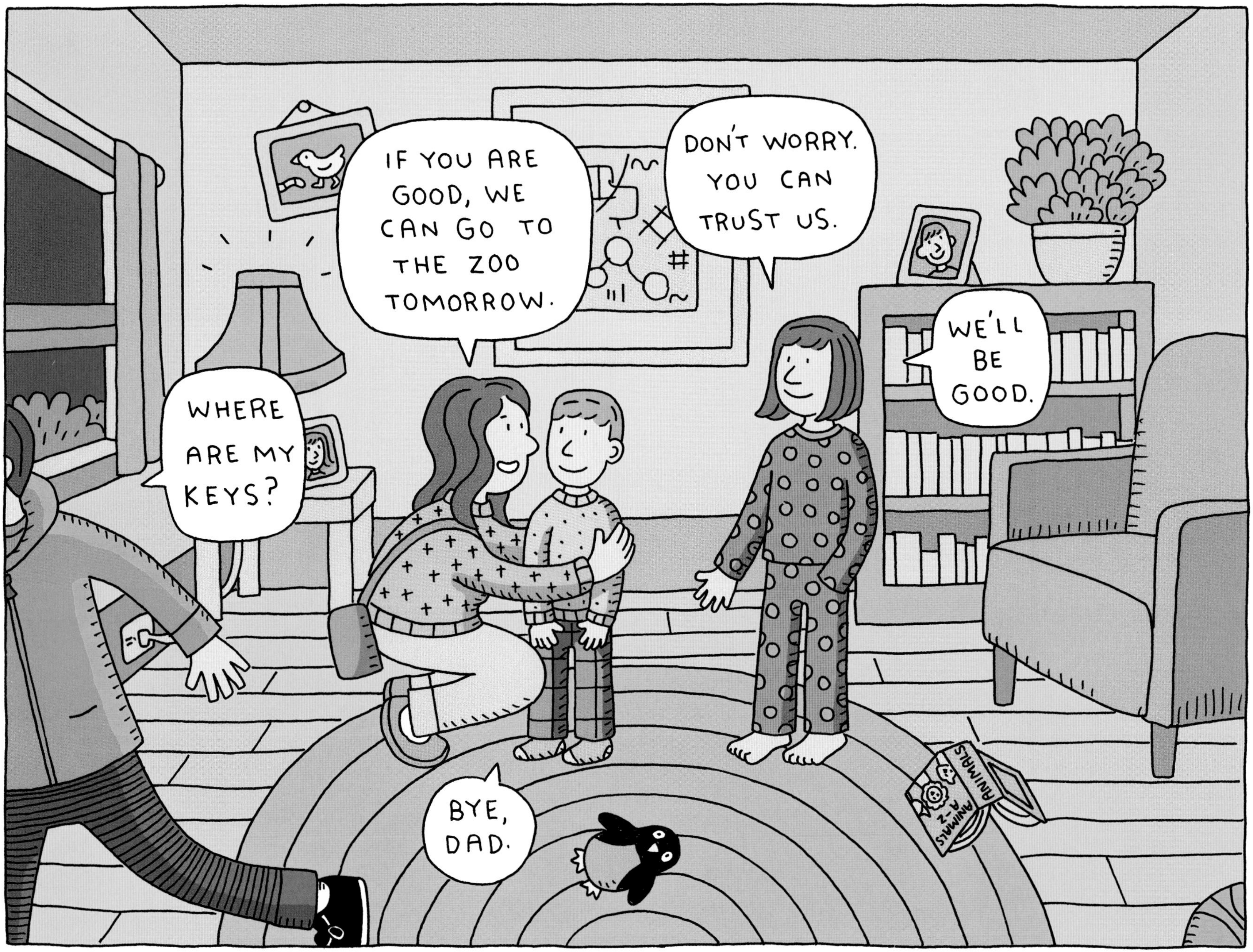
WHERE ARE MY KEYS?
IF YOU ARE GOOD, WE CAN GO TO THE ZOO TOMORROW.
DON'T WORRY. YOU CAN TRUST US.
WE'LL BE GOOD.
BYE, DAD.
ANIMALS
ANIMALS A-Z

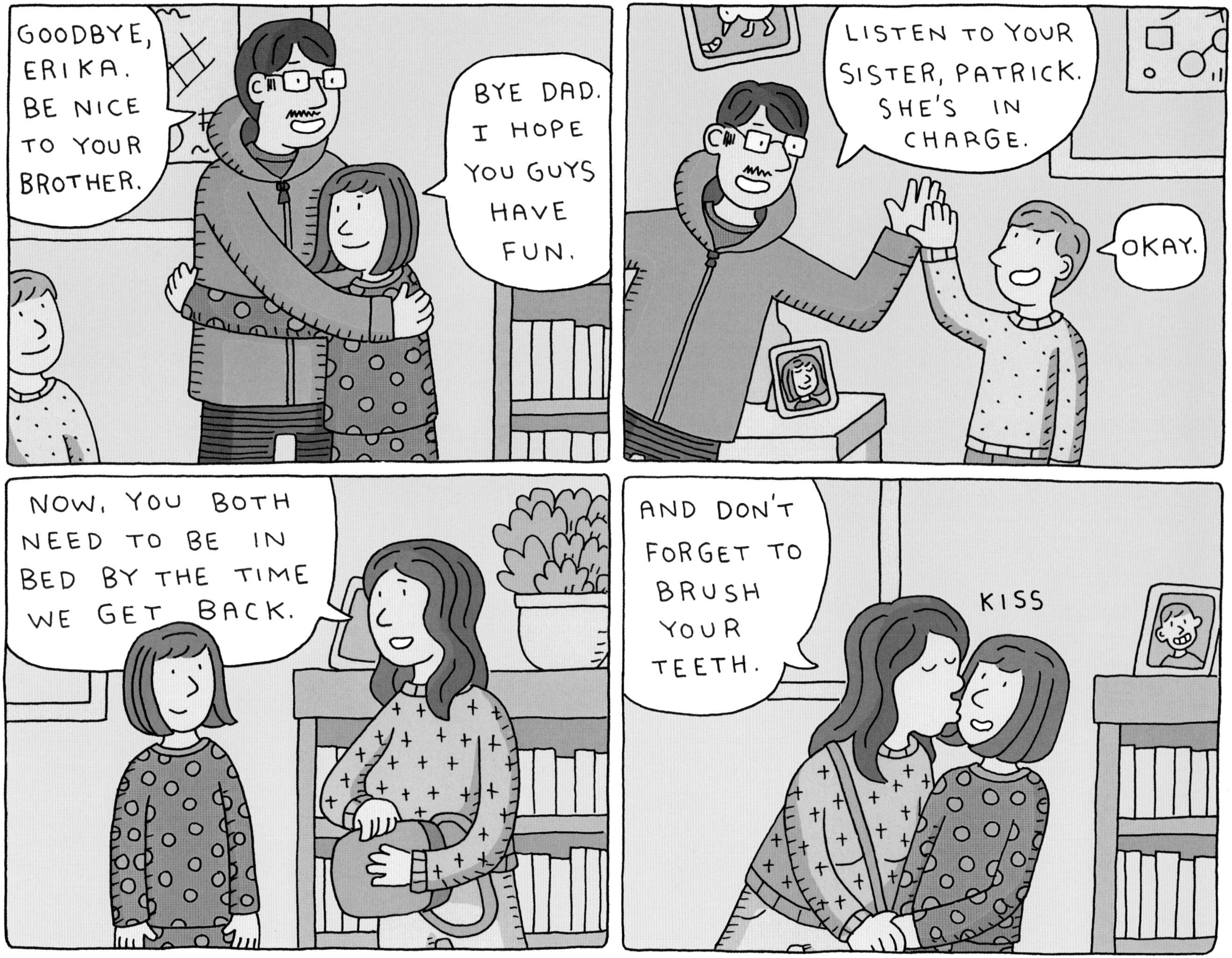
GOODBYE, ERIKA. BE NICE TO YOUR BROTHER.
BYE DAD. I HOPE YOU GUYS HAVE FUN.
LISTEN TO YOUR SISTER, PATRICK. SHE'S IN CHARGE.
OKAY.
NOW, YOU BOTH NEED TO BE IN BED BY THE TIME WE GET BACK.
AND DON'T FORGET TO BRUSH YOUR TEETH.
KISS

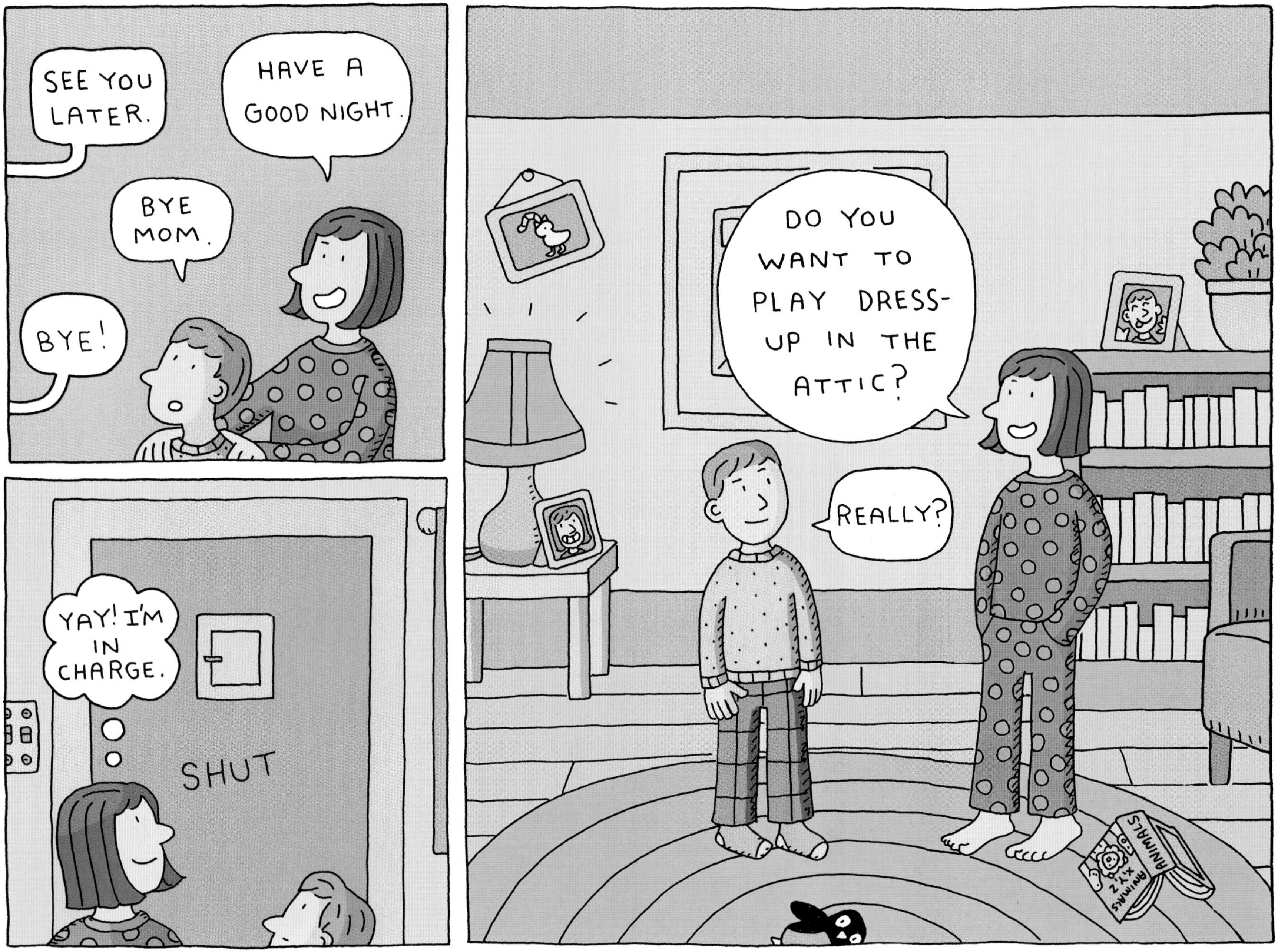
SEE YOU LATER.
HAVE A GOOD NIGHT.
BYE MOM.
BYE!
YAY! I'M IN CHARGE.
SHUT
DO YOU WANT TO PLAY DRESS-UP IN THE ATTIC?
REALLY?
ANIMALS

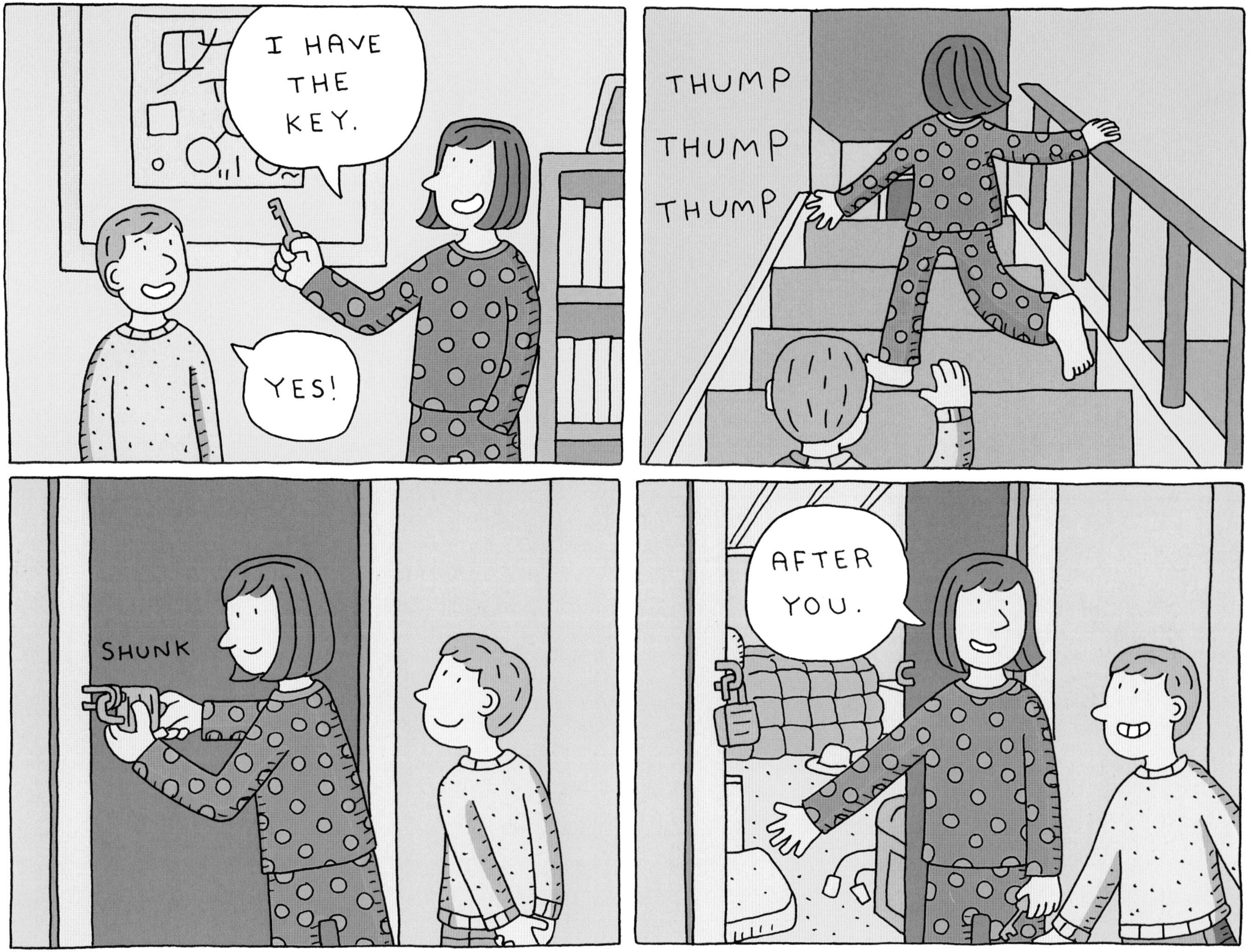
I HAVE THE KEY.
YES!
THUMP
THUMP
THUMP
SHUNK
AFTER YOU.

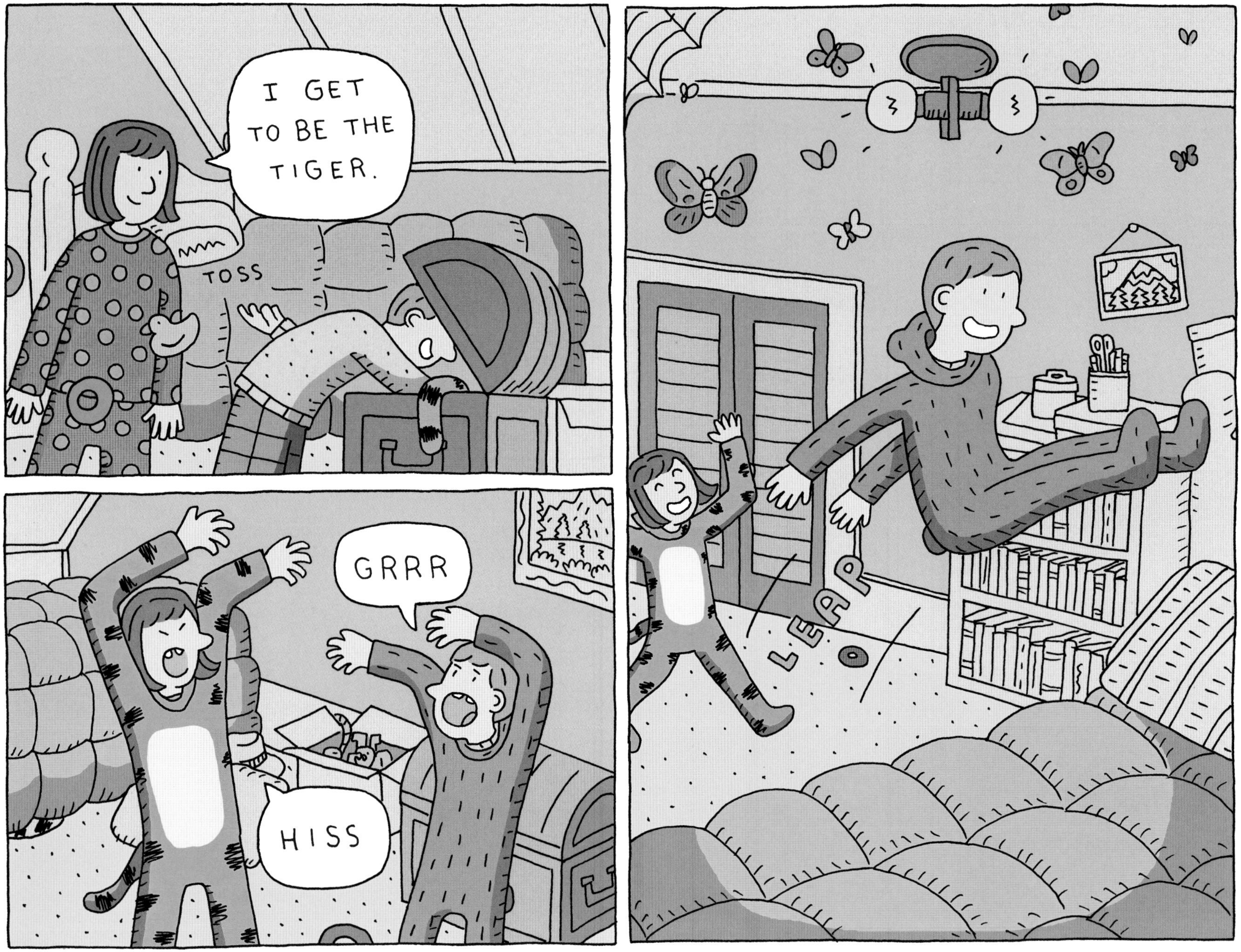
I GET TO BE THE TIGER.
TOSS
GRRR
HISS
LEAP

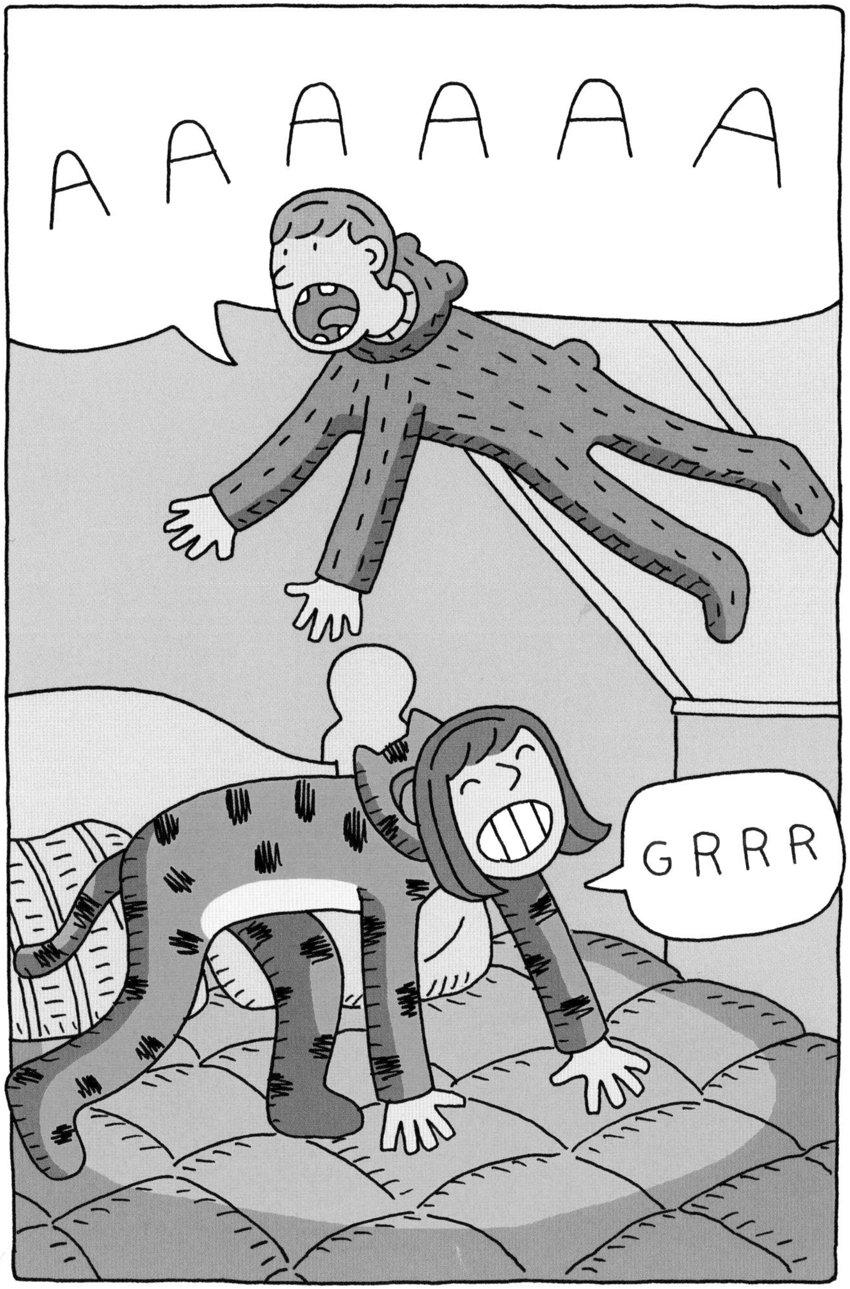
AAAAAA
GRRR

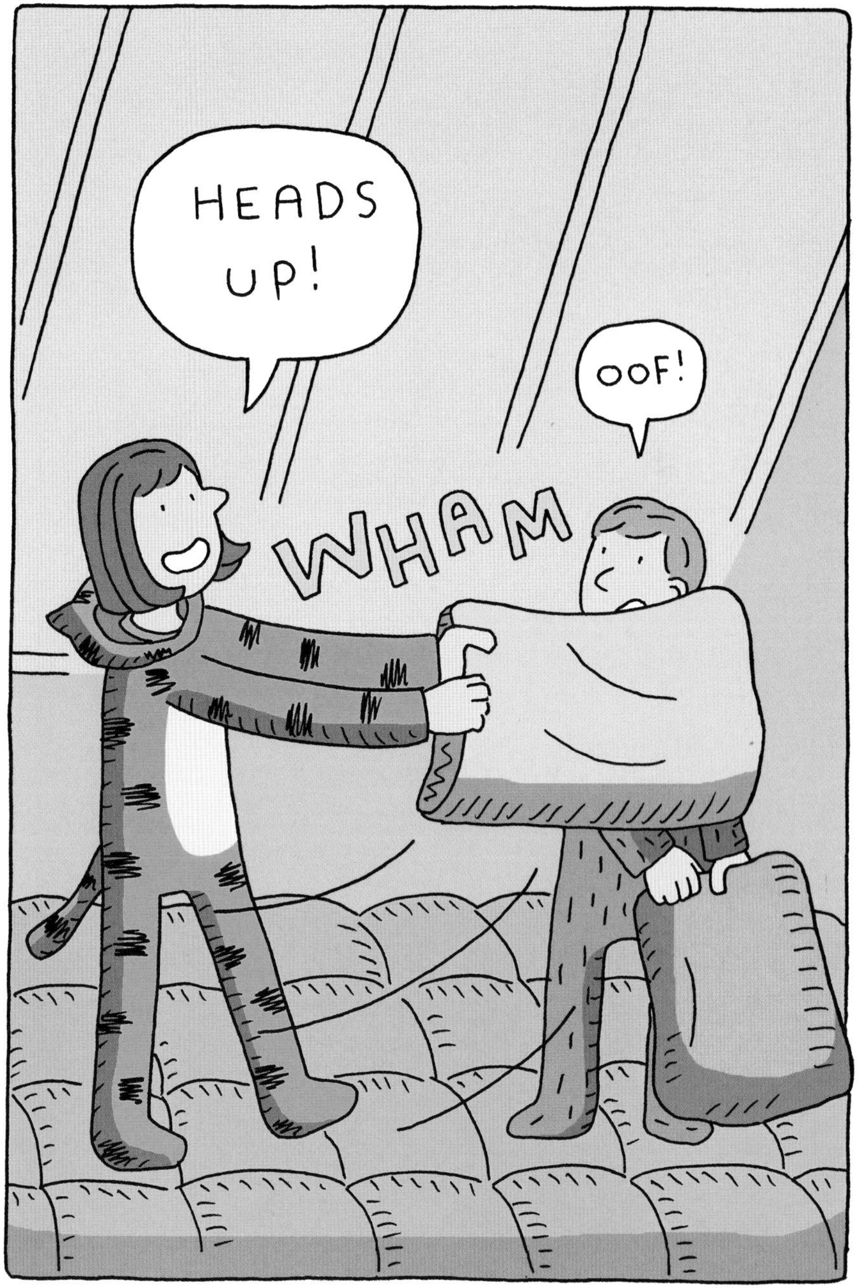
HEADS UP!
WHAM
OOF!

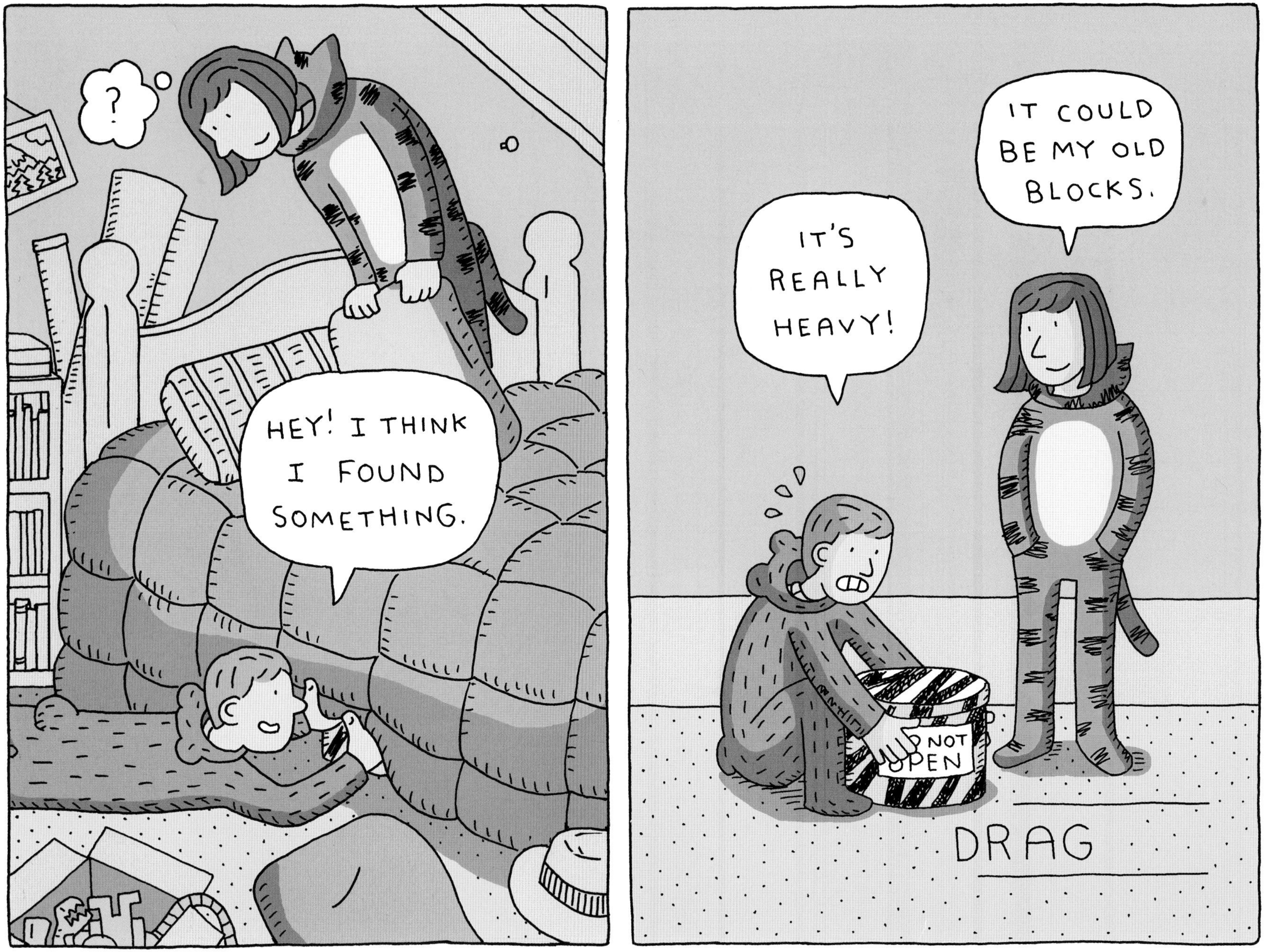
?
HEY! I THINK I FOUND SOMETHING.
IT'S REALLY HEAVY!
IT COULD BE MY OLD BLOCKS.
DRAG

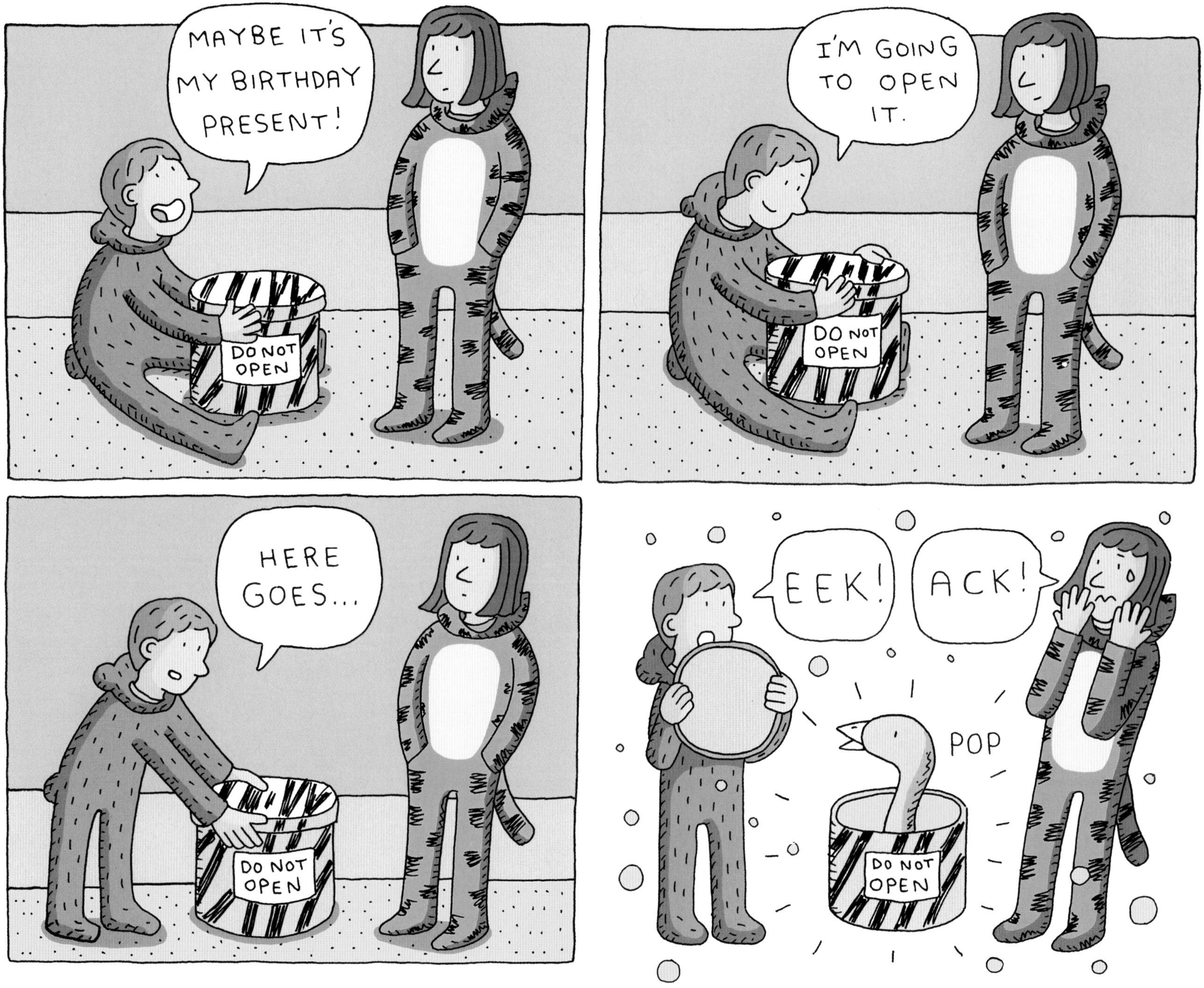
MAYBE IT'S MY BIRTHDAY PRESENT!
DO NOT OPEN
I'M GOING TO OPEN IT.
DO NOT OPEN
HERE GOES...
DO NOT OPEN
EEK!
ACK!
POP
DO NOT OPEN

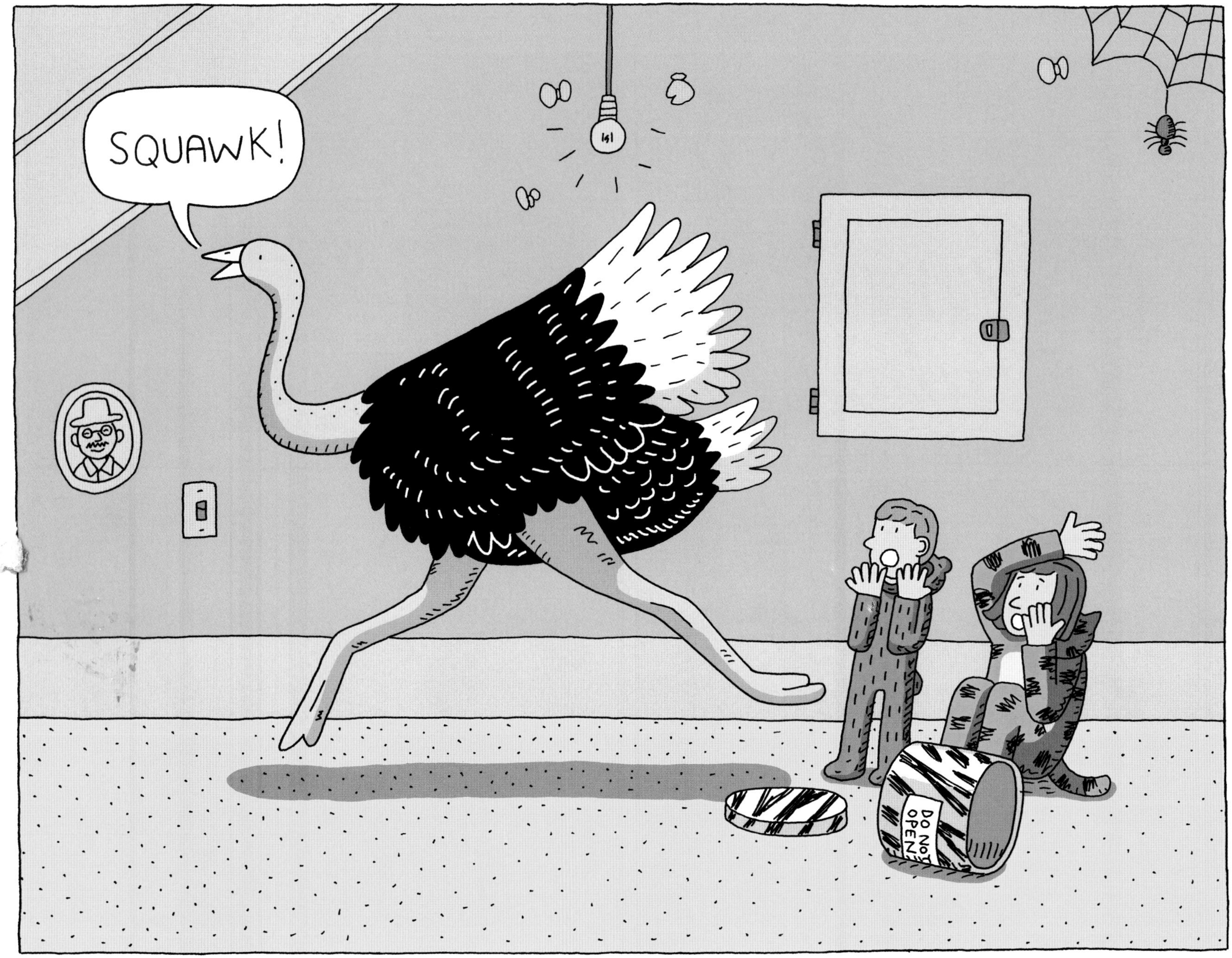
SQUAWK!
DO NOT OPEN

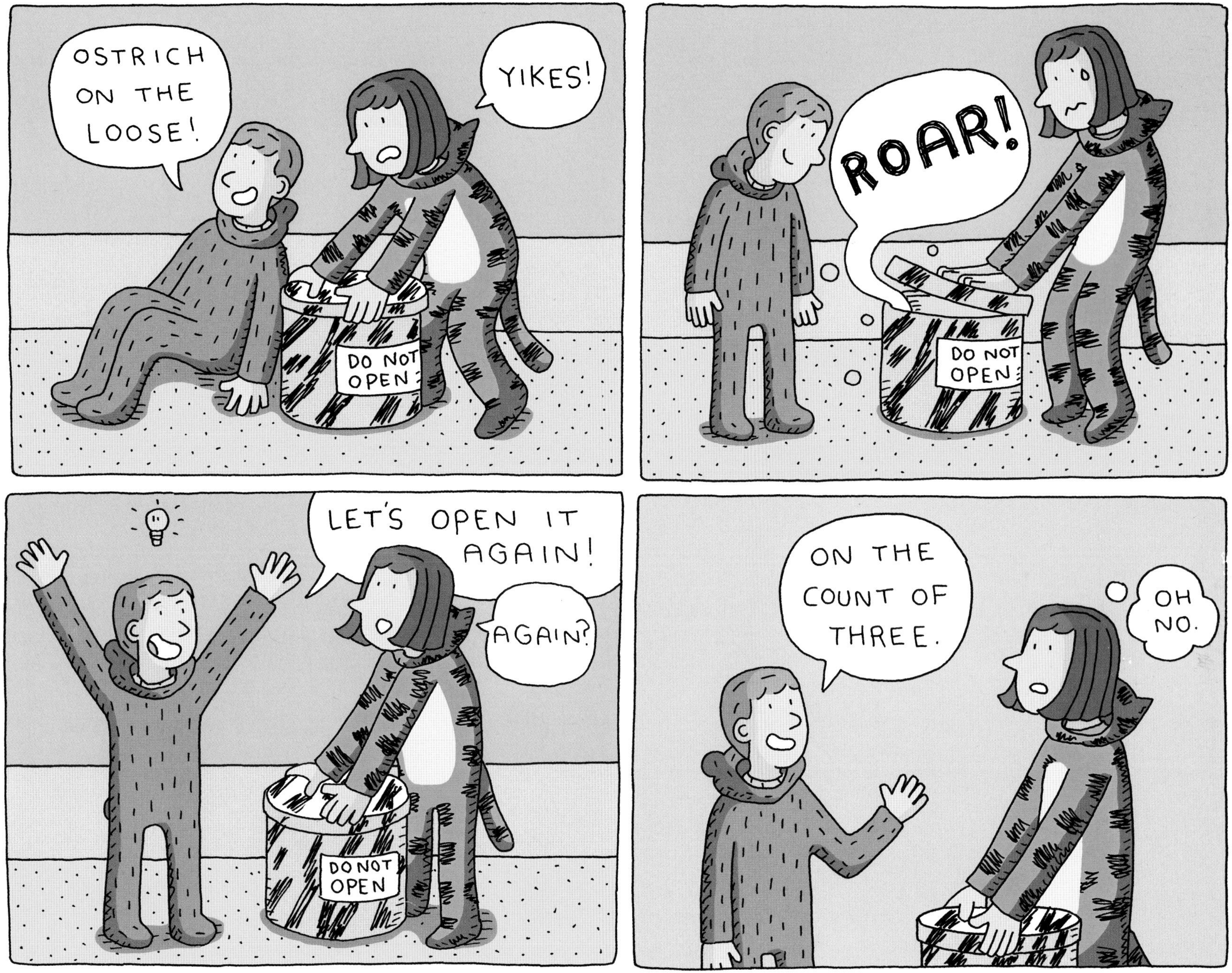
OSTRICH ON THE LOOSE!
YIKES!
ROAR!
DO NOT OPEN
LET'S OPEN IT AGAIN!
AGAIN?
DO NOT OPEN
DO NOT OPEN
ON THE COUNT OF THREE.
OH NO.

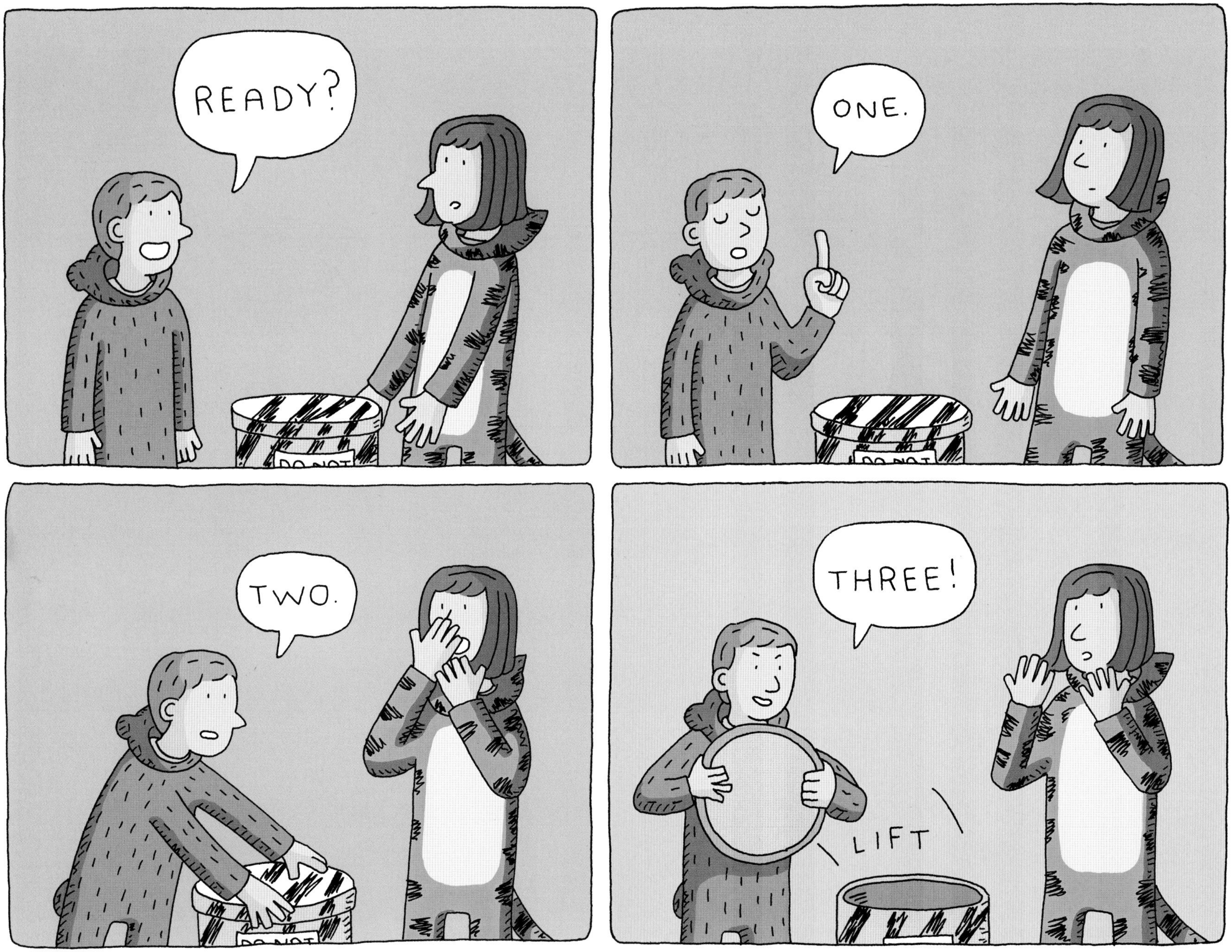
READY?
ONE.
TWO.
THREE!
LIFT

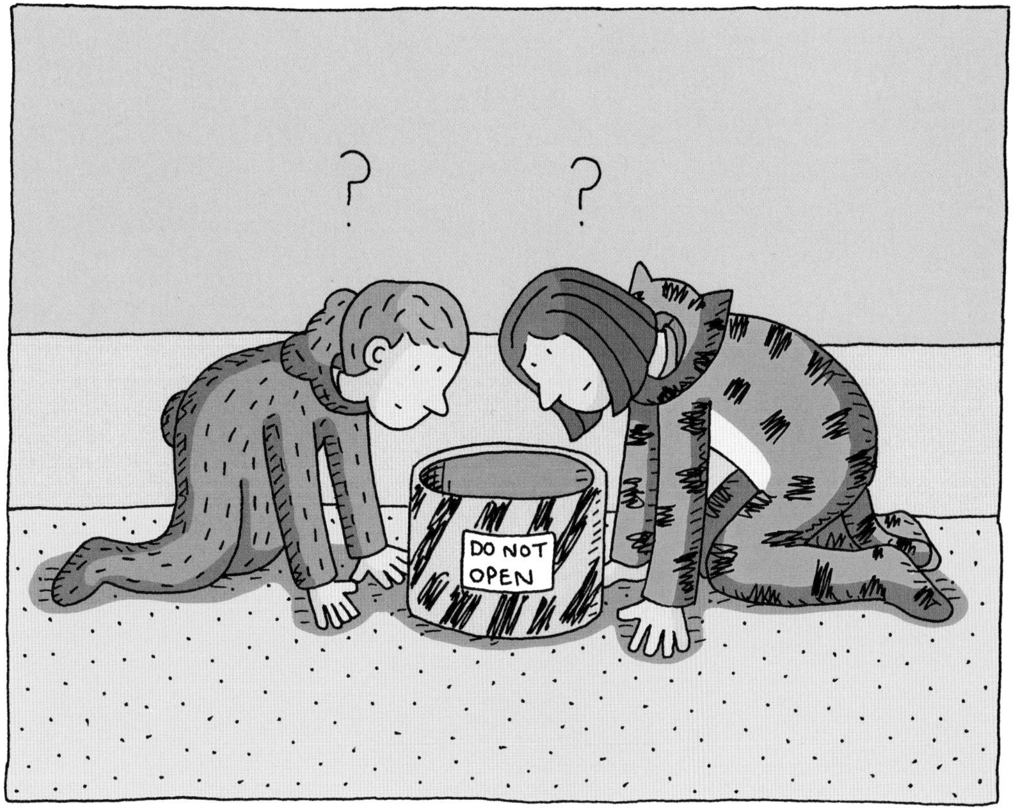
?
?
DO NOT OPEN

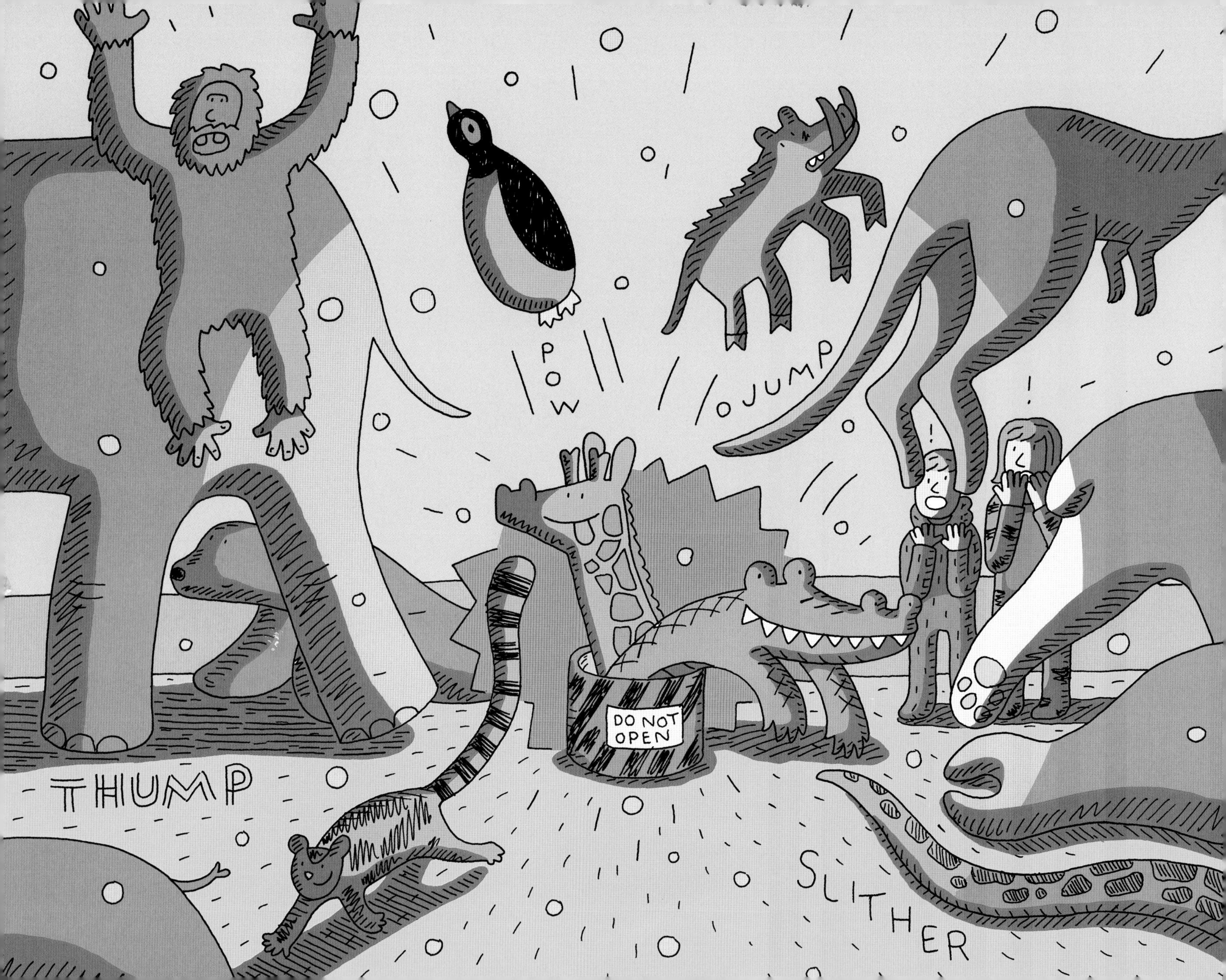
POW
JUMP
DO NOT OPEN
THUMP
SLITHER

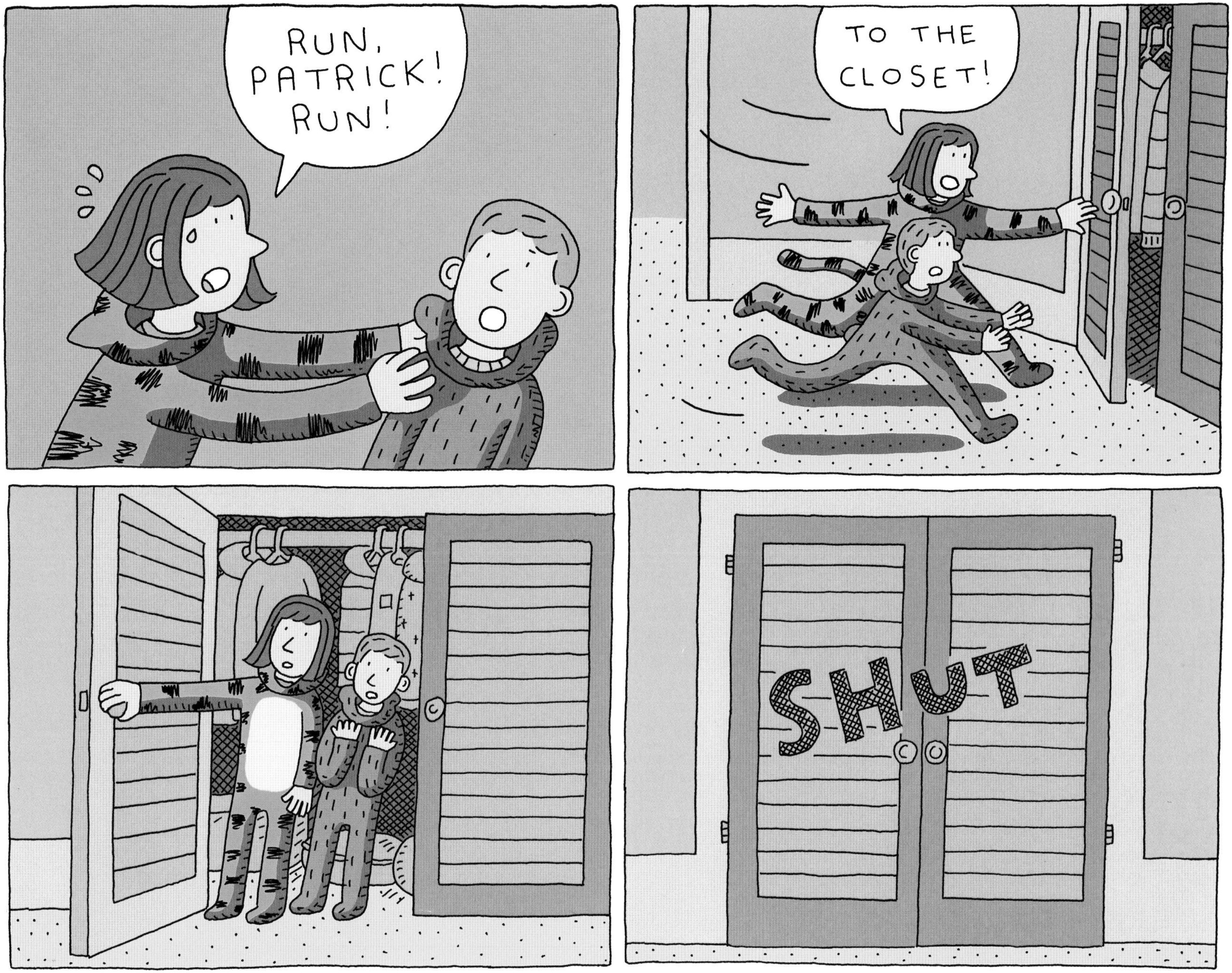
RUN, PATRICK! RUN!
TO THE CLOSET!
SHUT

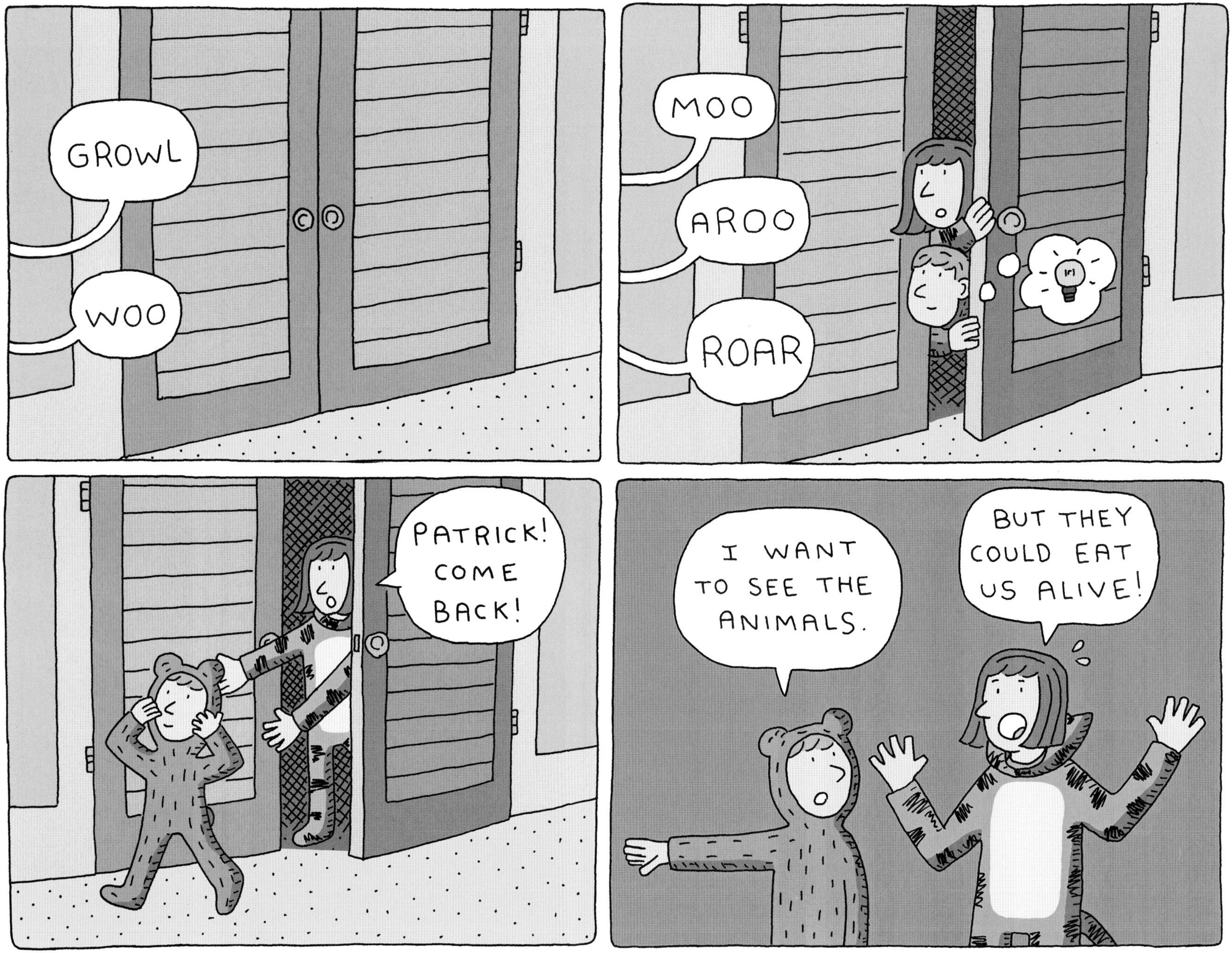
GROWL
WOO
MOO
AROO
ROAR
PATRICK! COME BACK!
I WANT TO SEE THE ANIMALS.
BUT THEY COULD EAT US ALIVE!

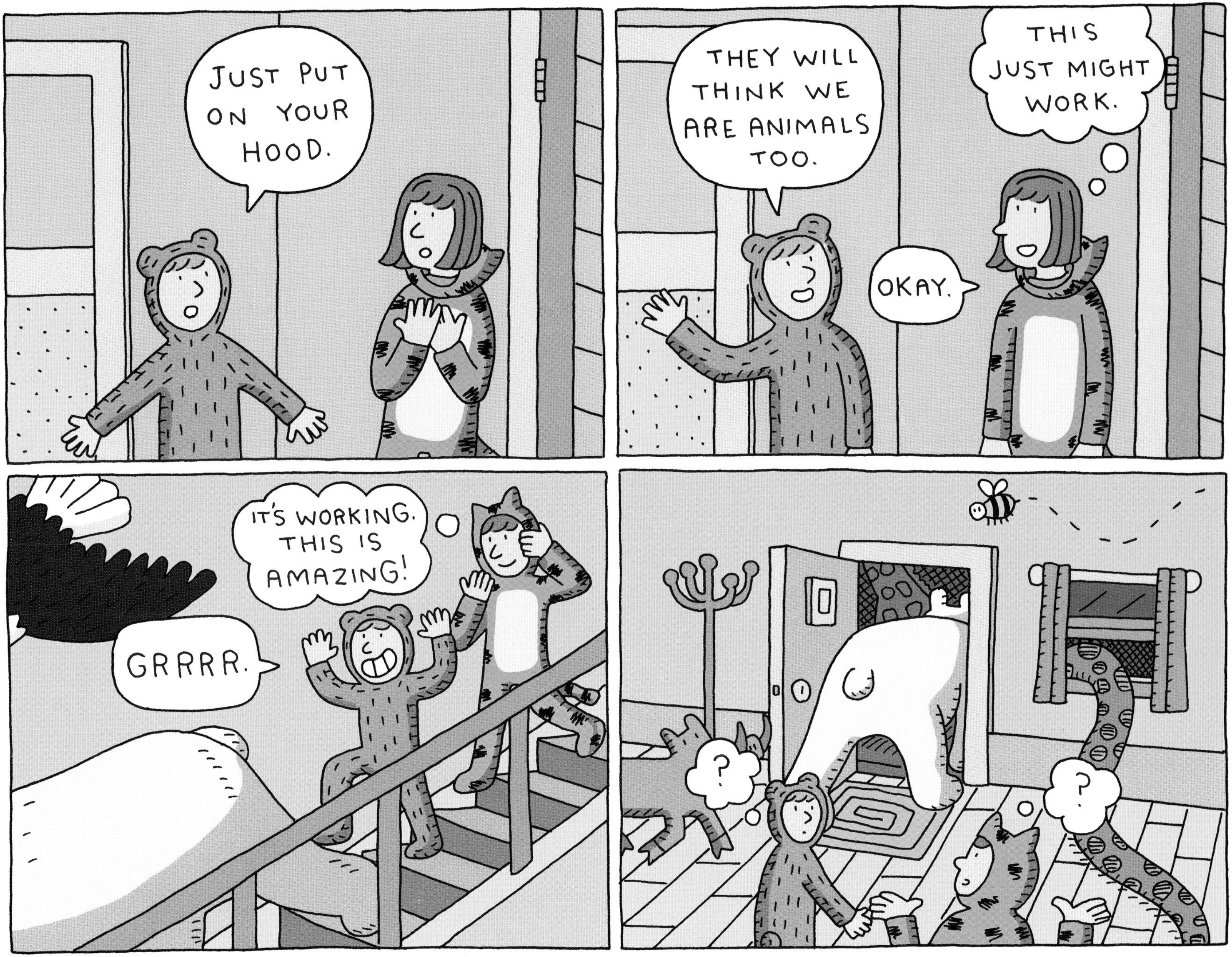
JUST PUT ON YOUR HOOD.
THEY WILL THINK WE ARE ANIMALS TOO.
OKAY.
THIS JUST MIGHT WORK.
GRRRR.
IT'S WORKING. THIS IS AMAZING!
?
?

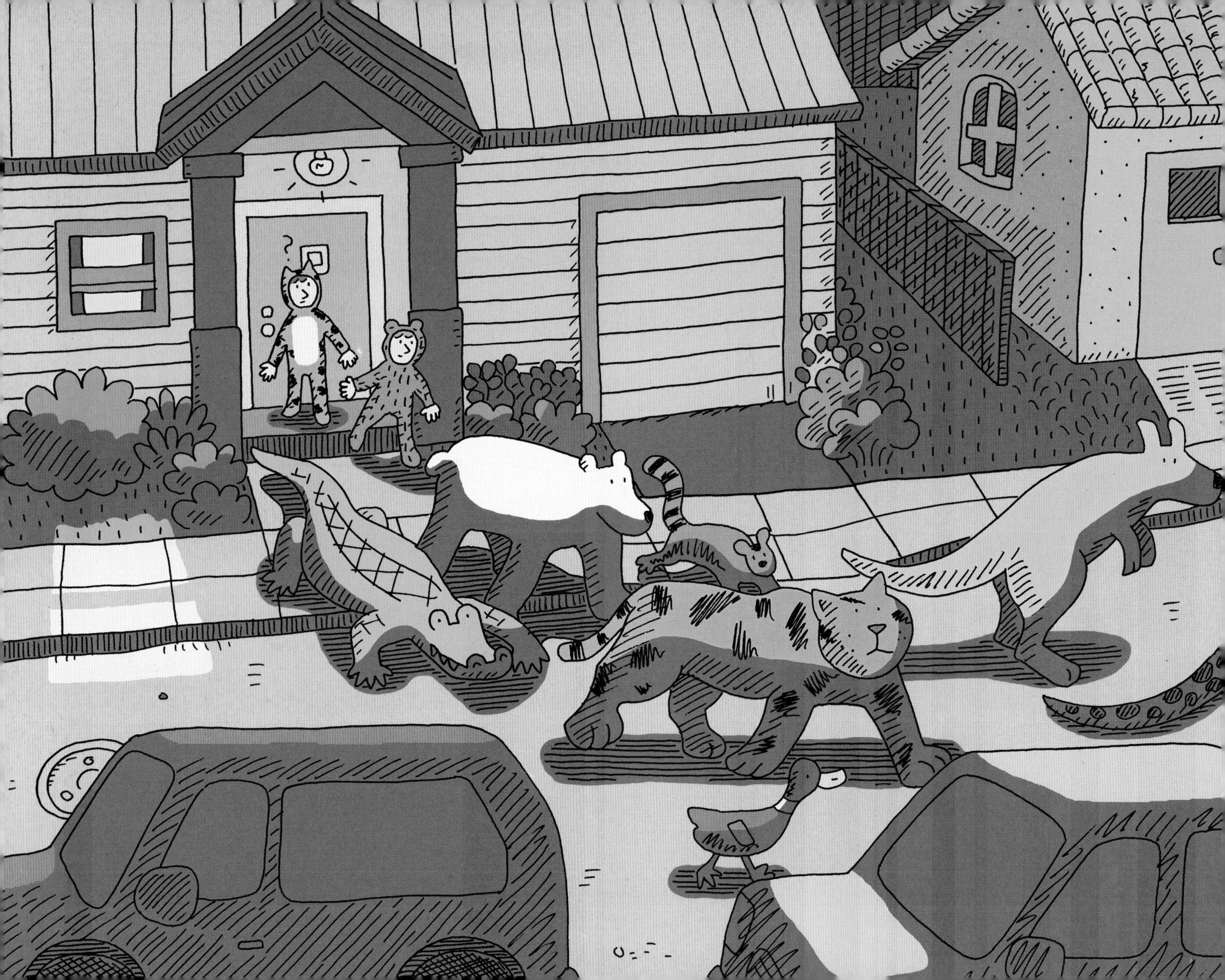

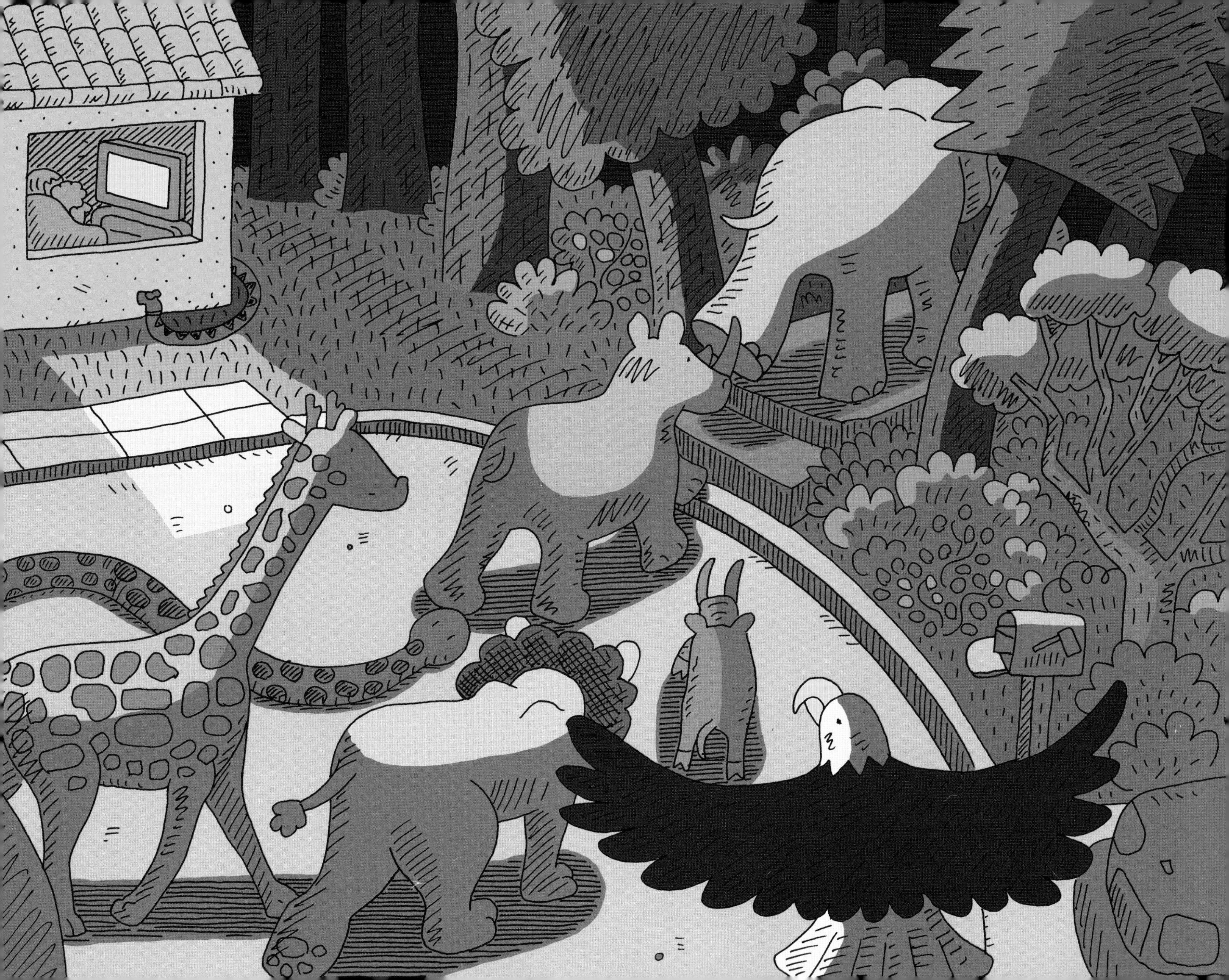

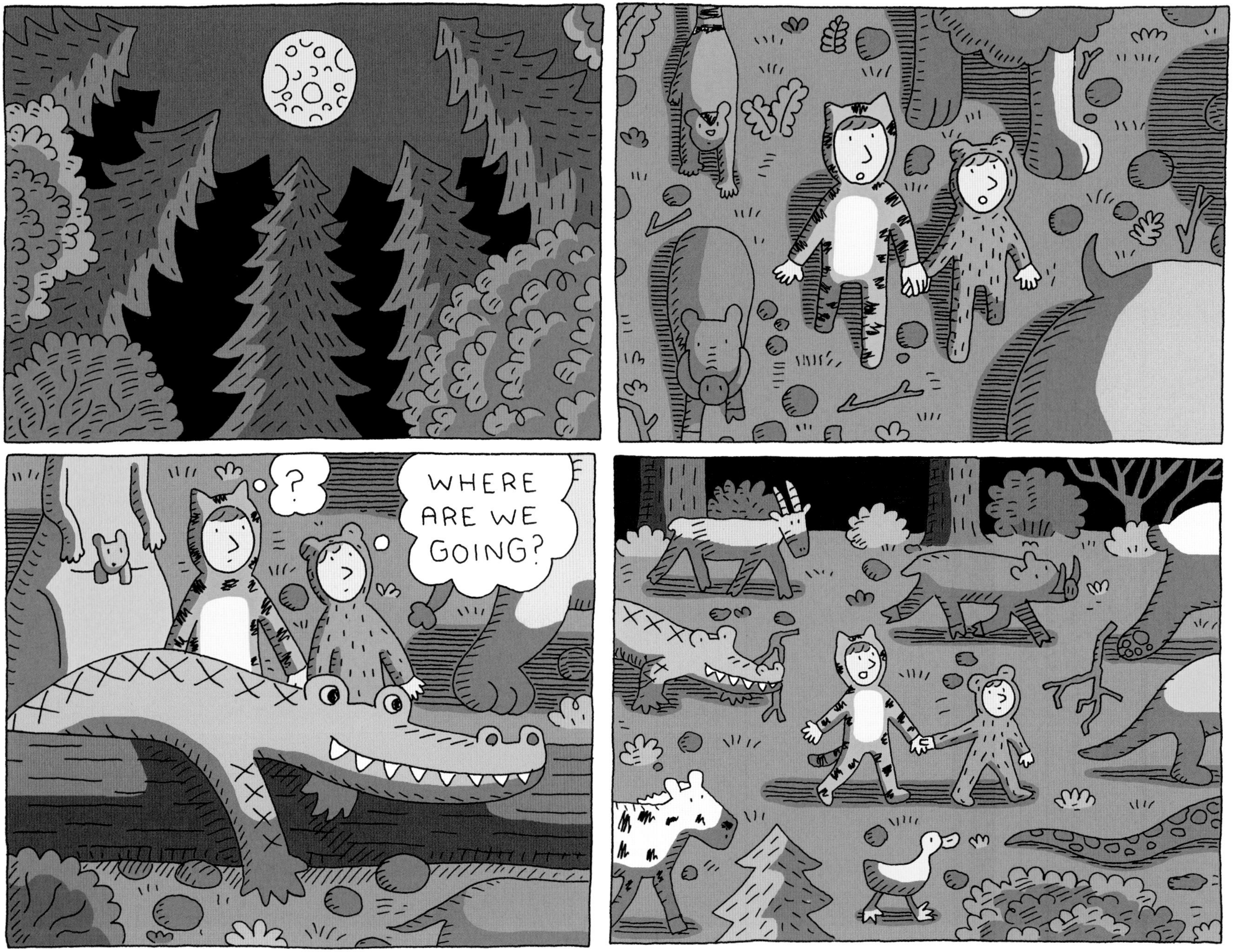
?
WHERE ARE WE GOING?

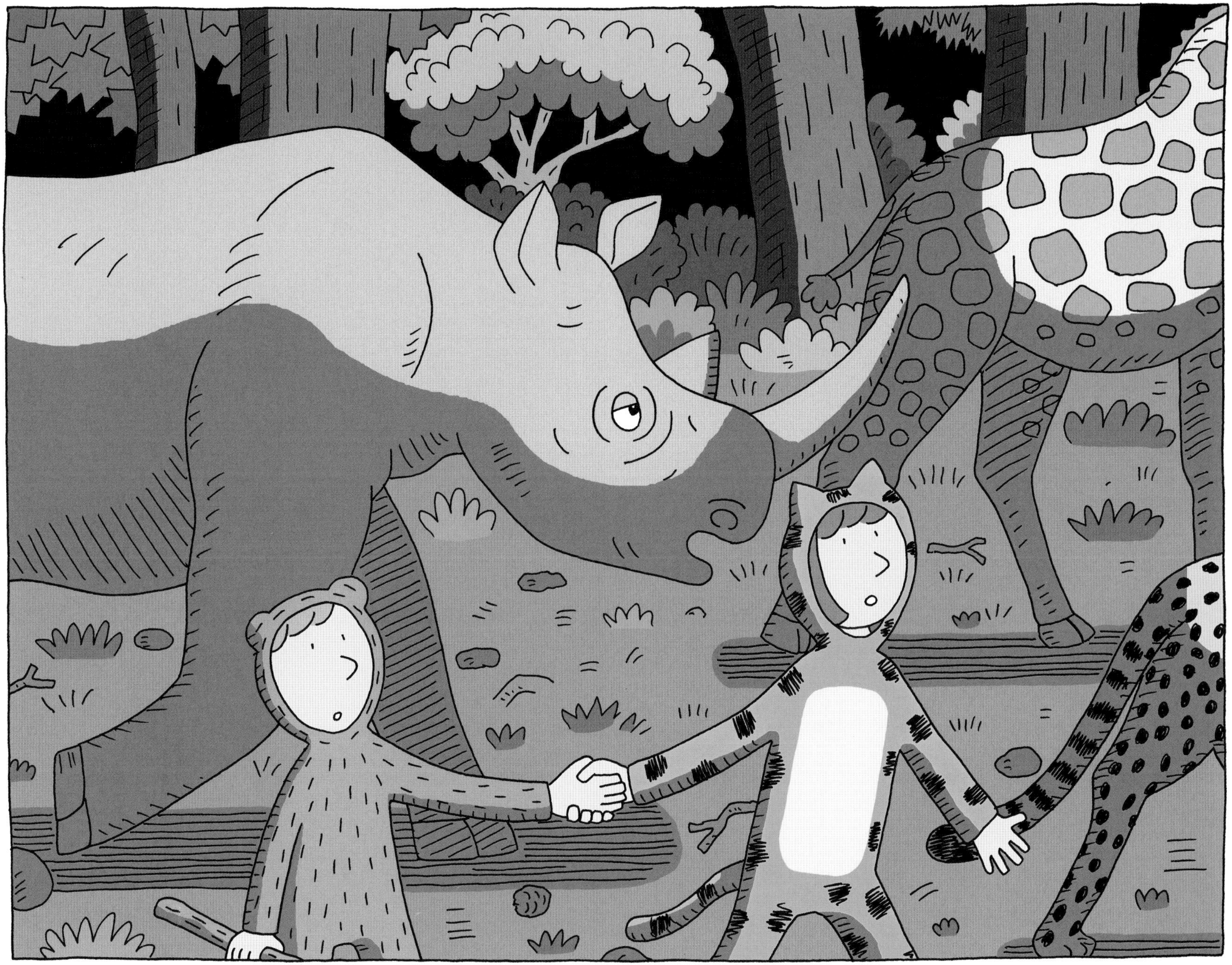

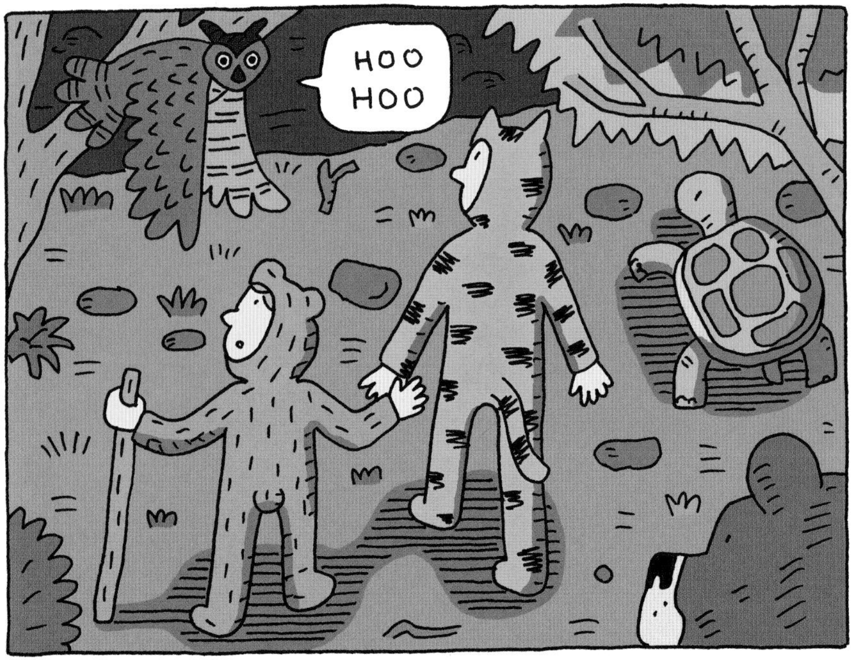
HOO HOO
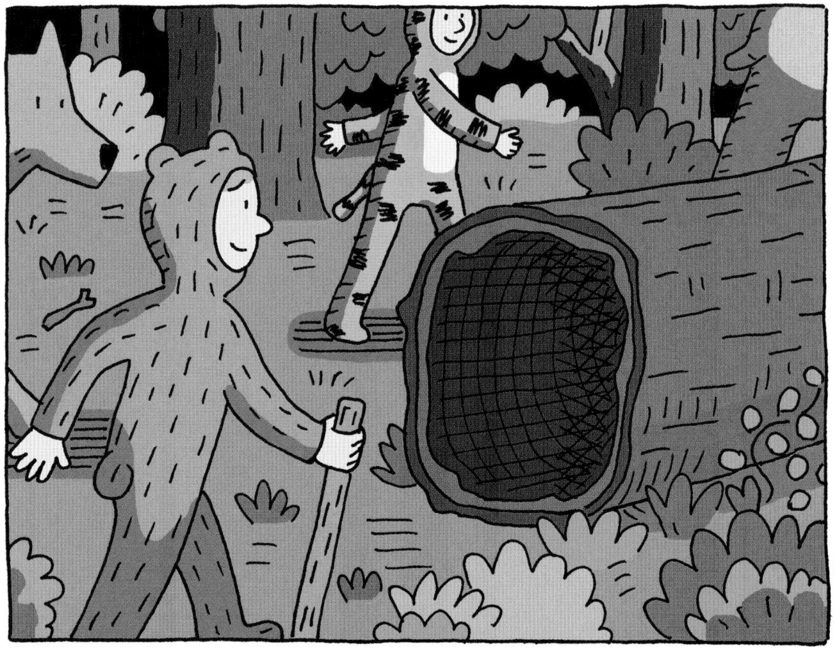
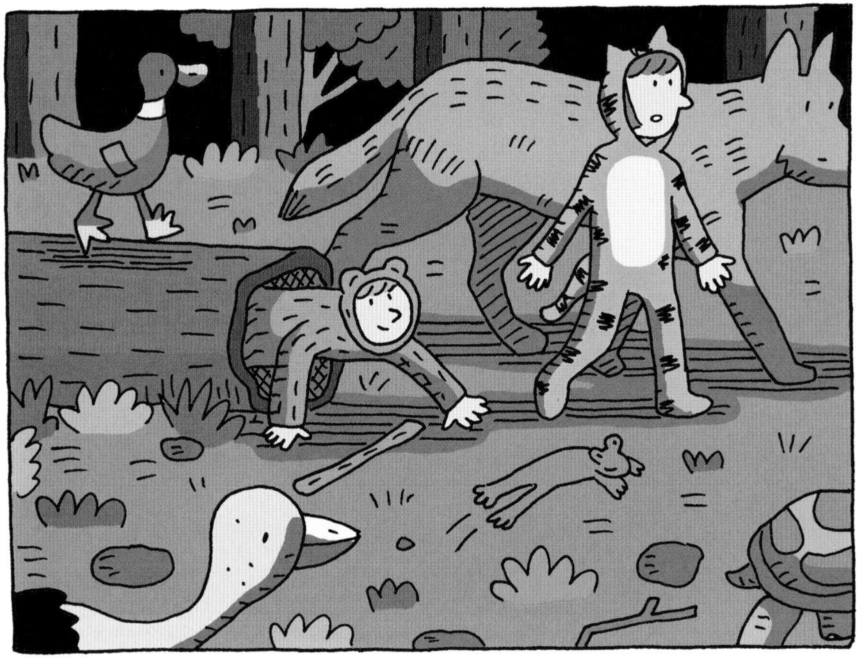
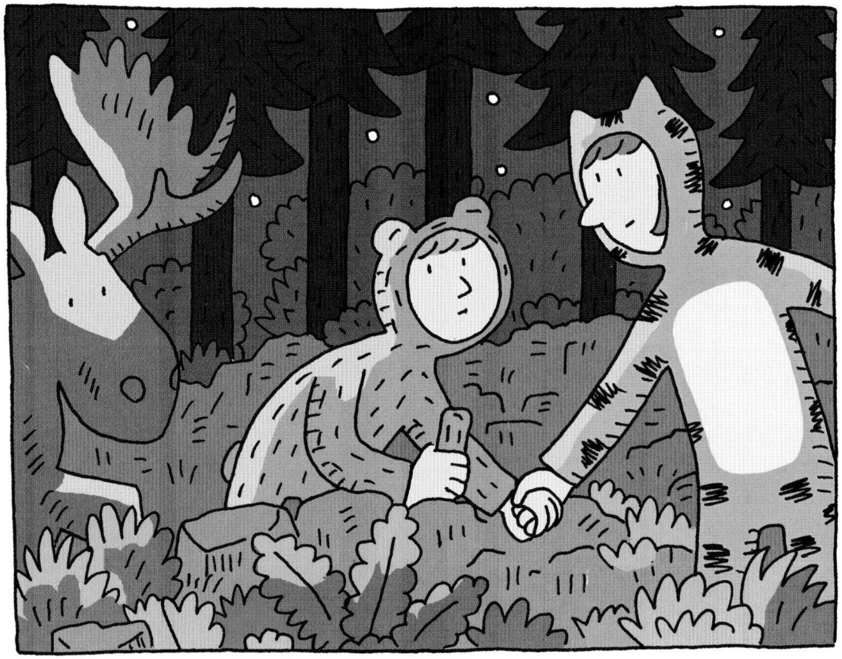

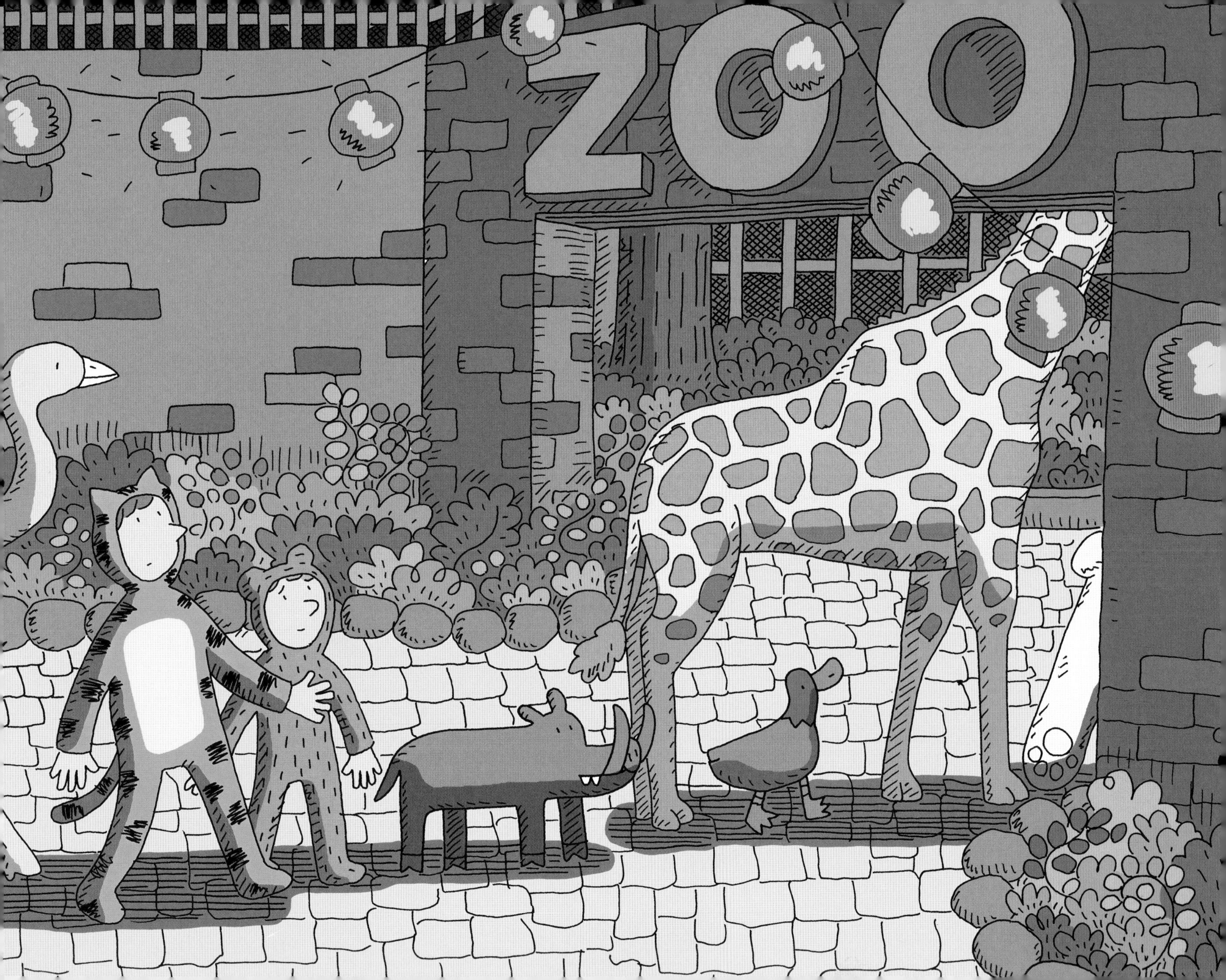
ZOO

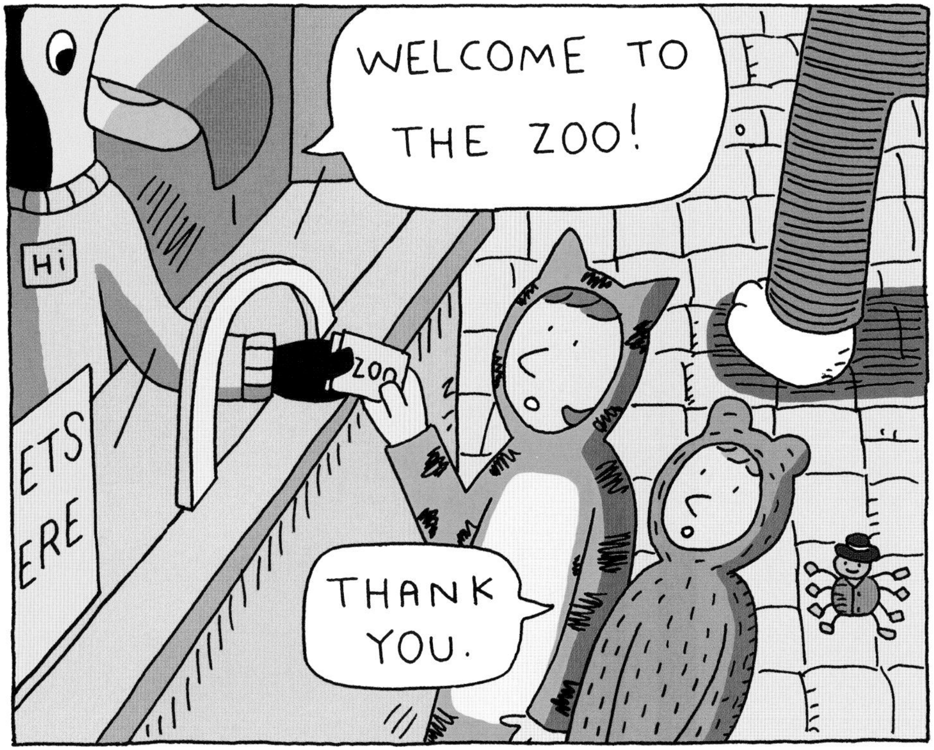
WELCOME TO THE ZOO!
Hi
ZOO
ETS ERE
THANK YOU.

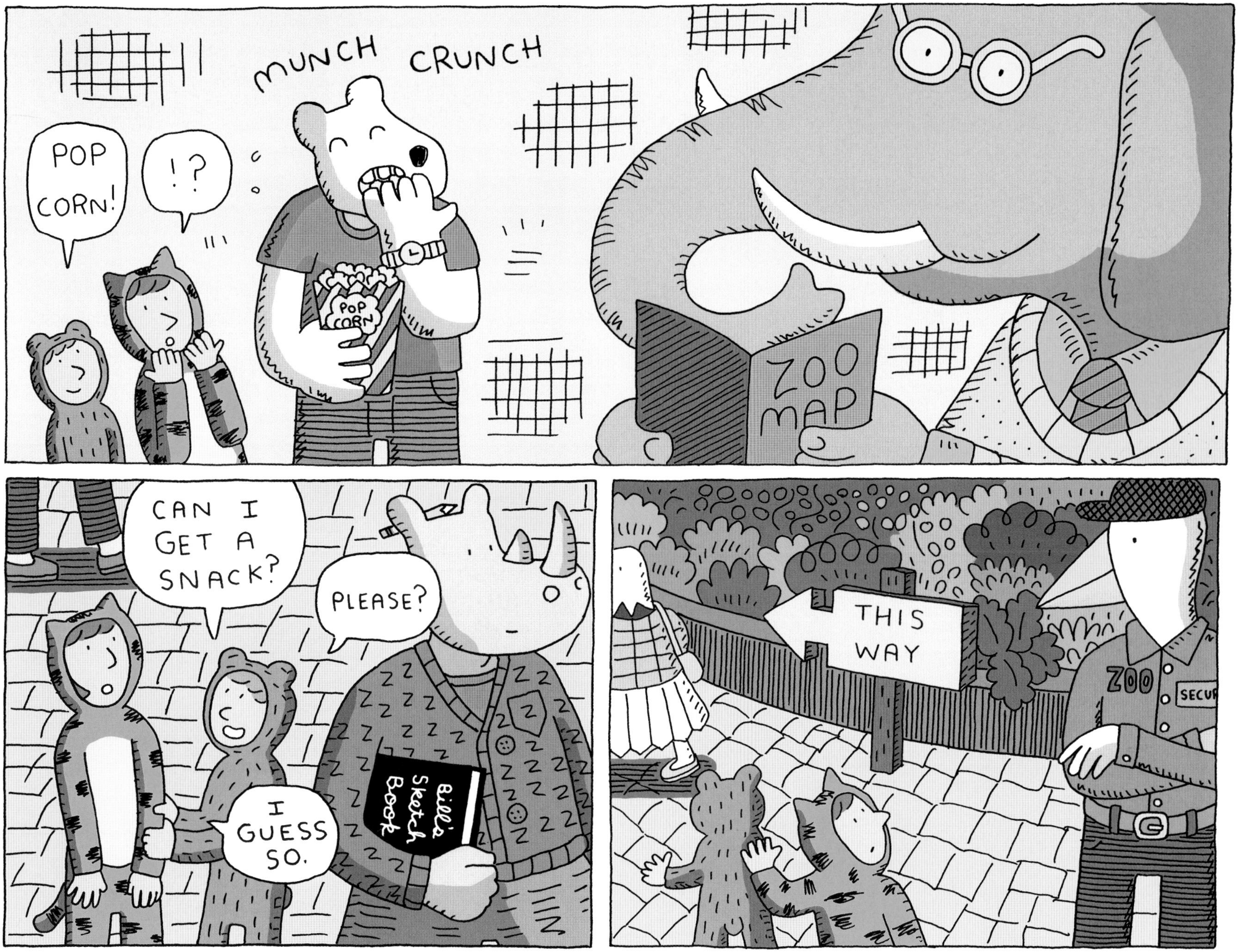
POP CORN!
!?
MUNCH CRUNCH
POP CORN
ZOO MAP
CAN I GET A SNACK?
PLEASE?
I GUESS SO.
Bill's Sketch Book
THIS WAY
ZOO

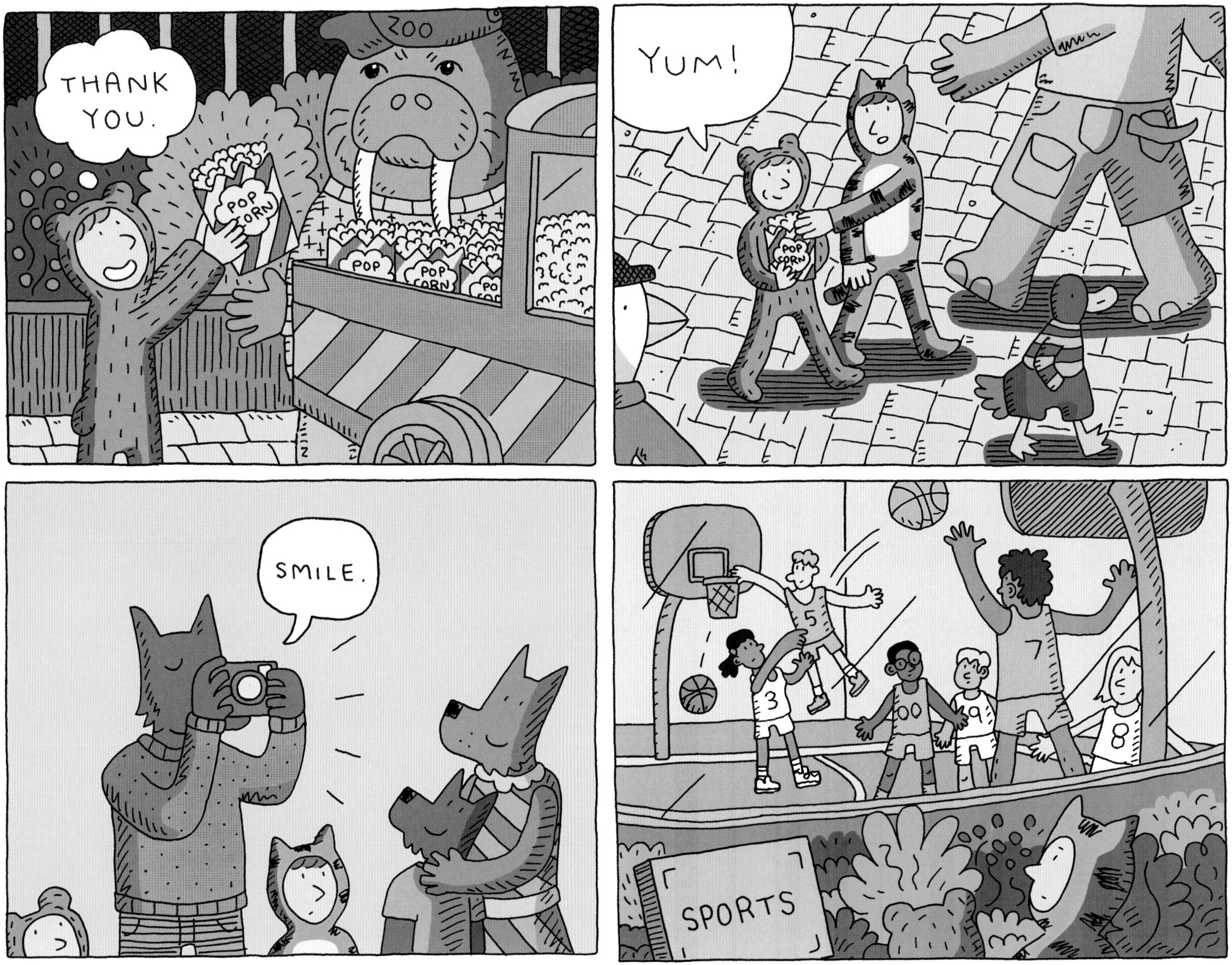
THANK YOU.
ZOO
POP CORN
POP
POP CORN
YUM!
POP CORN
SMILE.
SPORTS

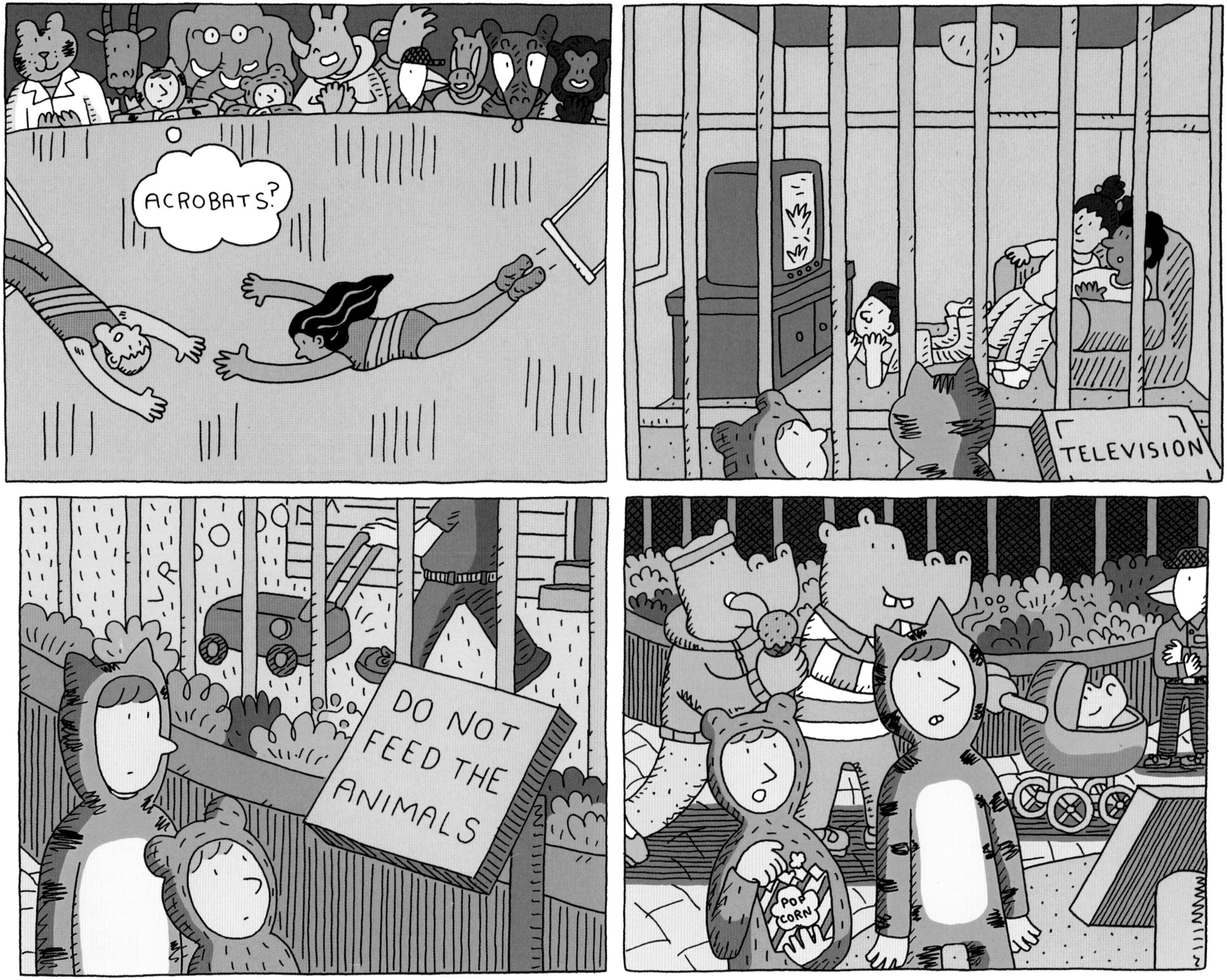

ACROBATS?
TELEVISION
DO NOT FEED THE ANIMALS
POP CORN

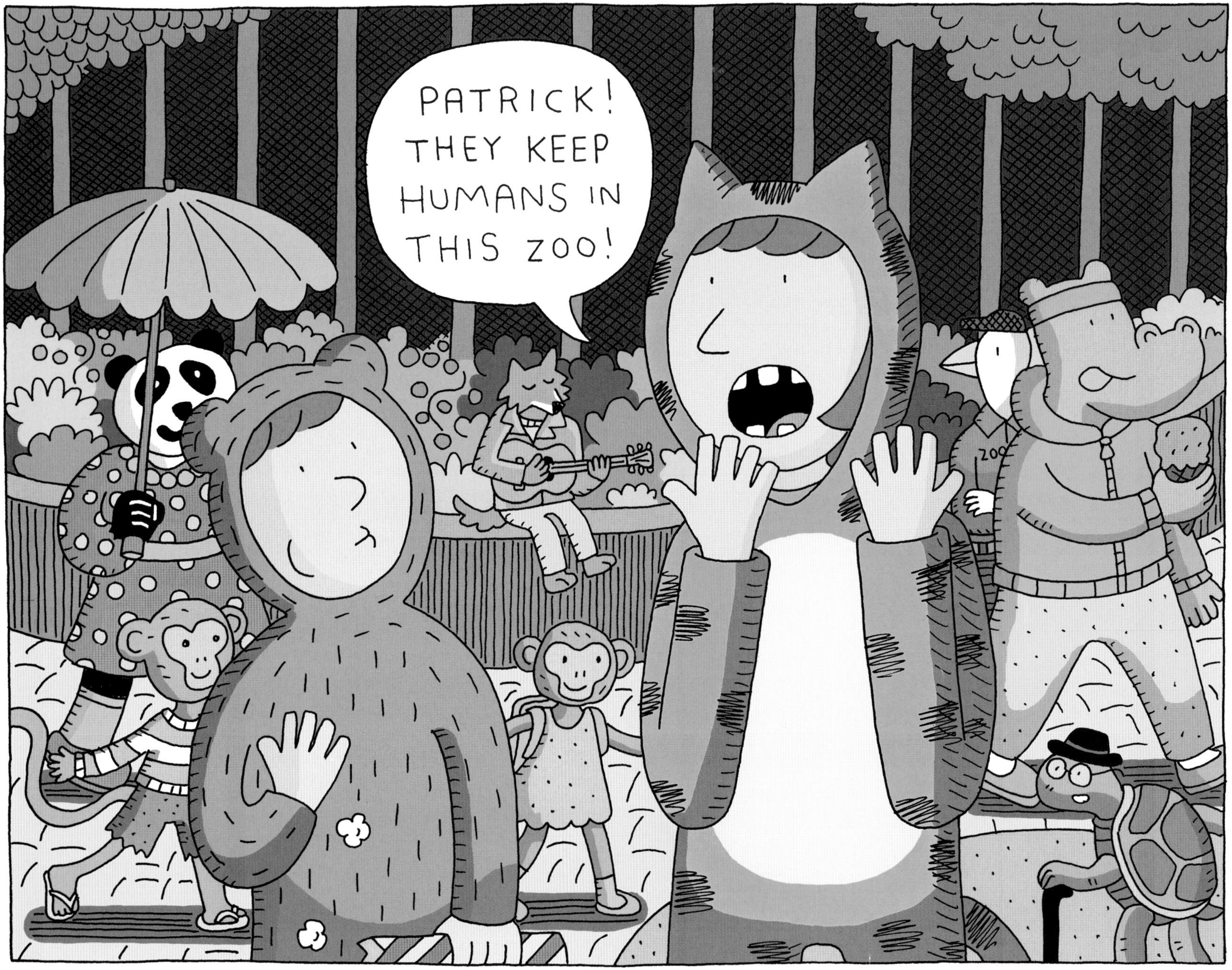
PATRICK! THEY KEEP HUMANS IN THIS ZOO!

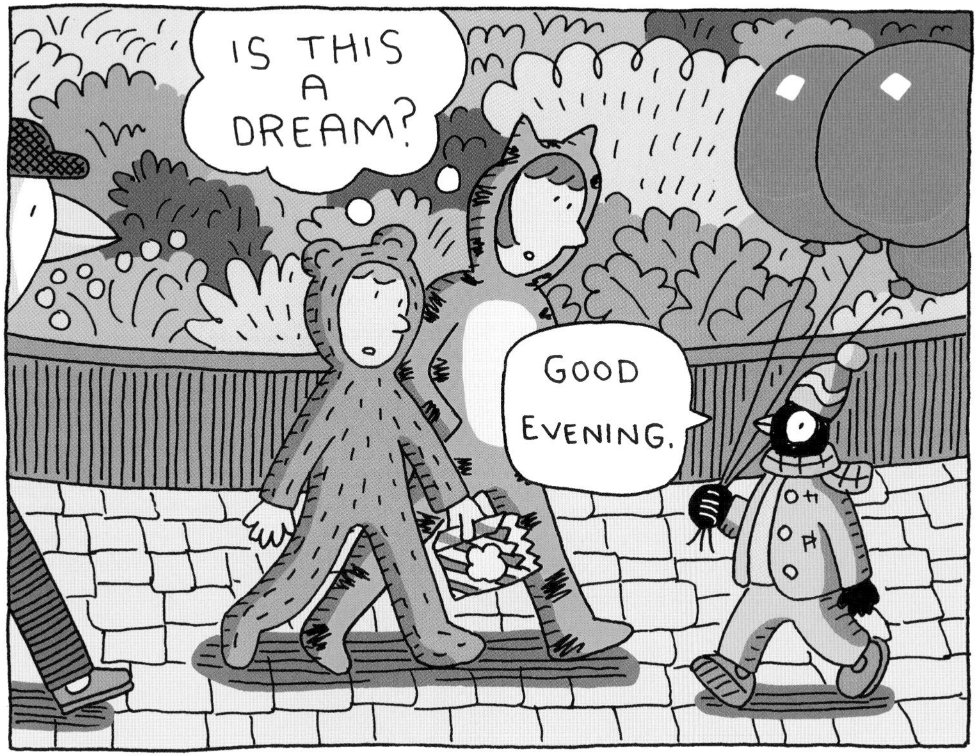
IS THIS A DREAM?
GOOD EVENING.

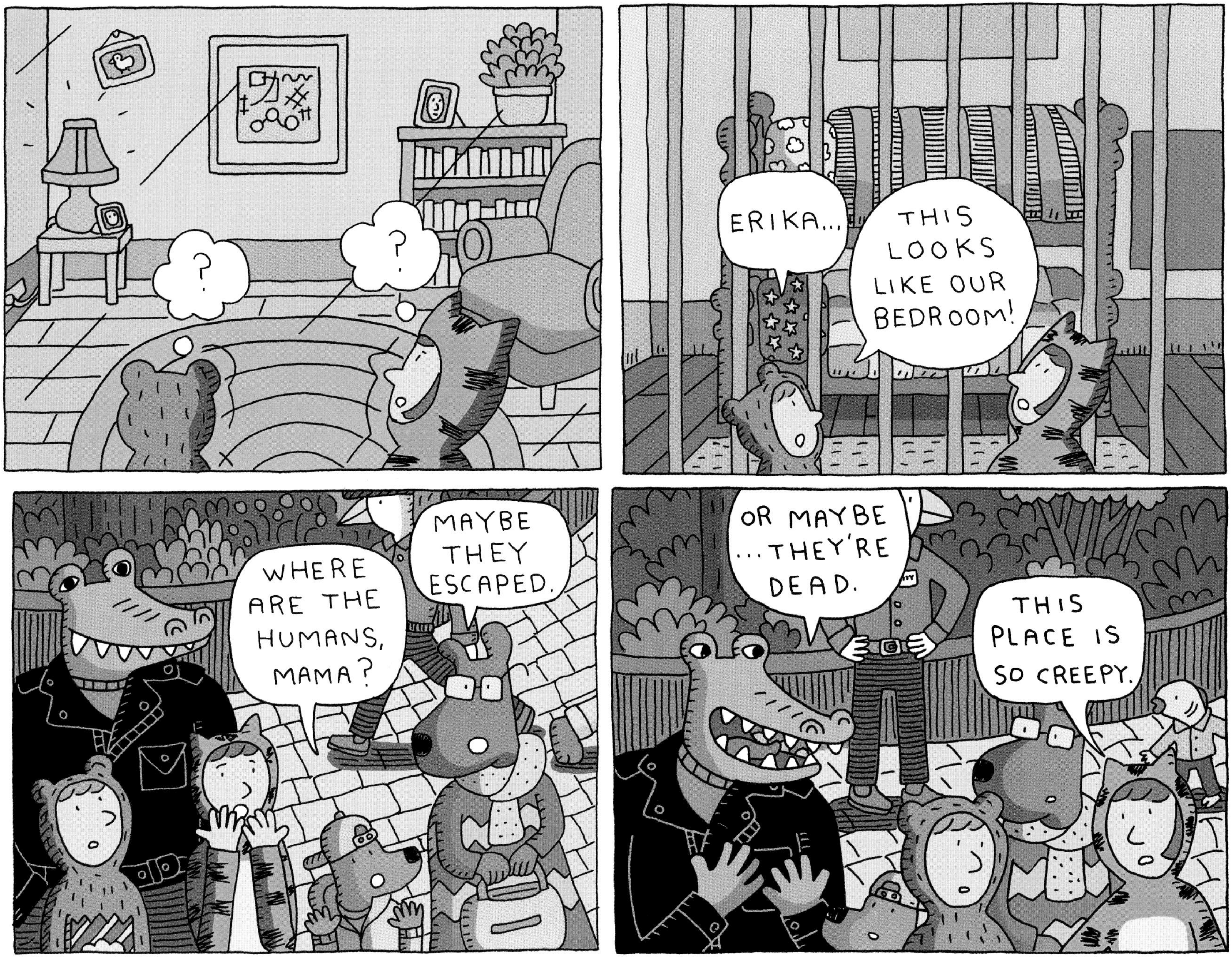
?
?
ERIKA...
THIS LOOKS LIKE OUR BEDROOM!
WHERE ARE THE HUMANS, MAMA?
MAYBE THEY ESCAPED.
OR MAYBE ...THEY'RE DEAD.
THIS PLACE IS SO CREEPY.

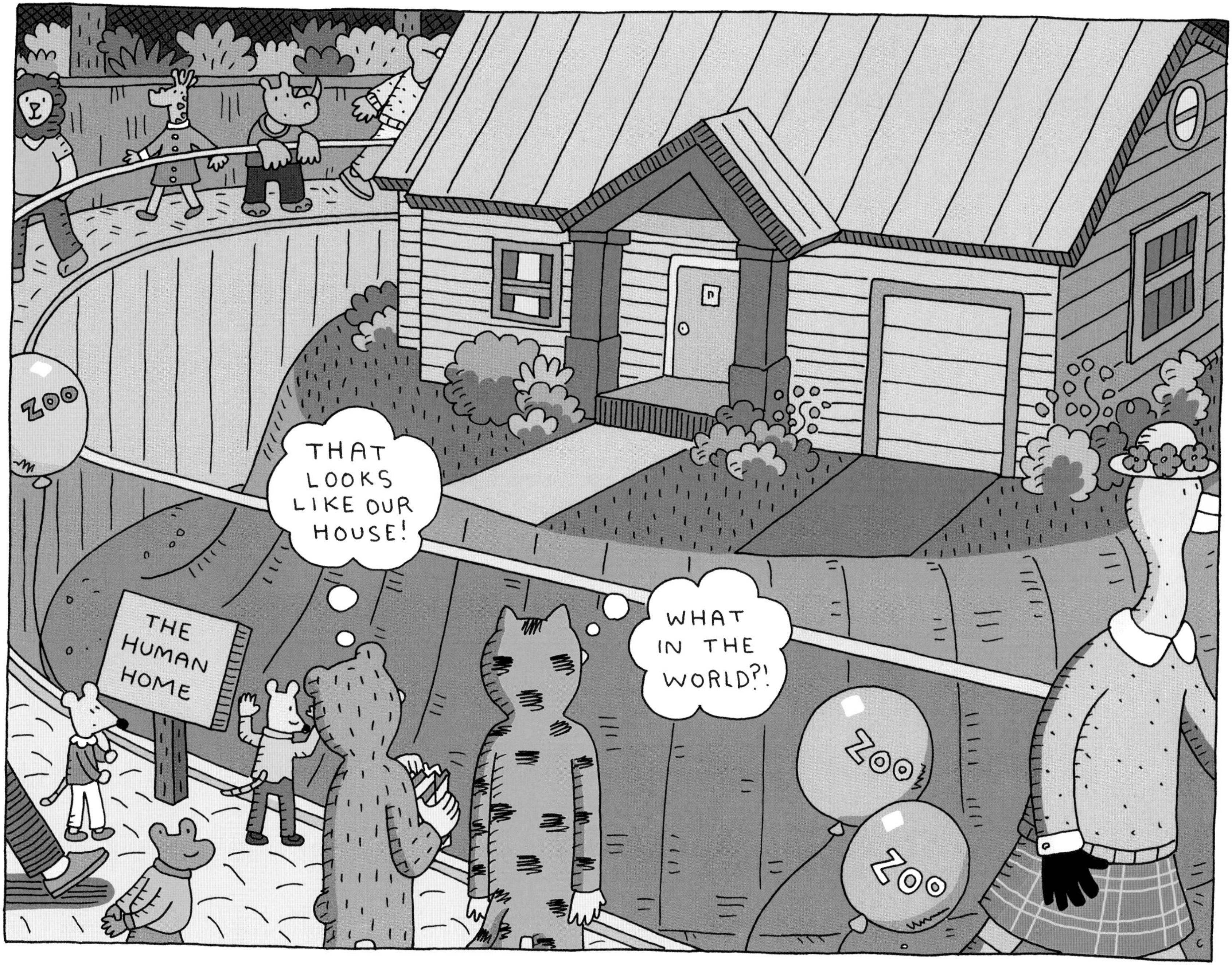
THAT LOOKS LIKE OUR HOUSE!
WHAT IN THE WORLD?!
THE HUMAN HOME
ZOO
ZOO
ZOO

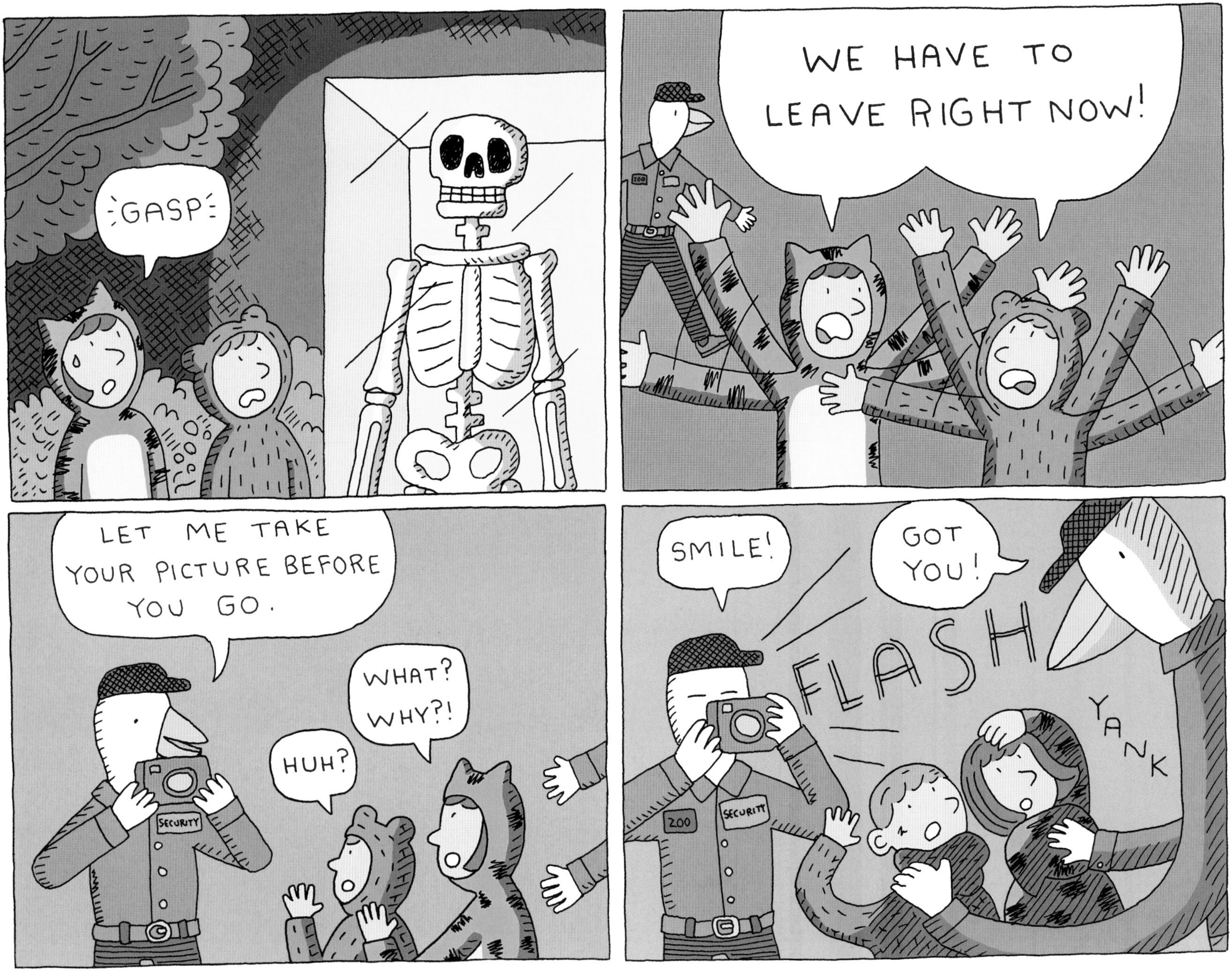
GASP
WE HAVE TO LEAVE RIGHT NOW!
LET ME TAKE YOUR PICTURE BEFORE YOU GO.
SECURITY
WHAT? WHY?!
HUH?
SMILE!
GOT YOU!
FLASH
ZOO
SECURITY
YANK

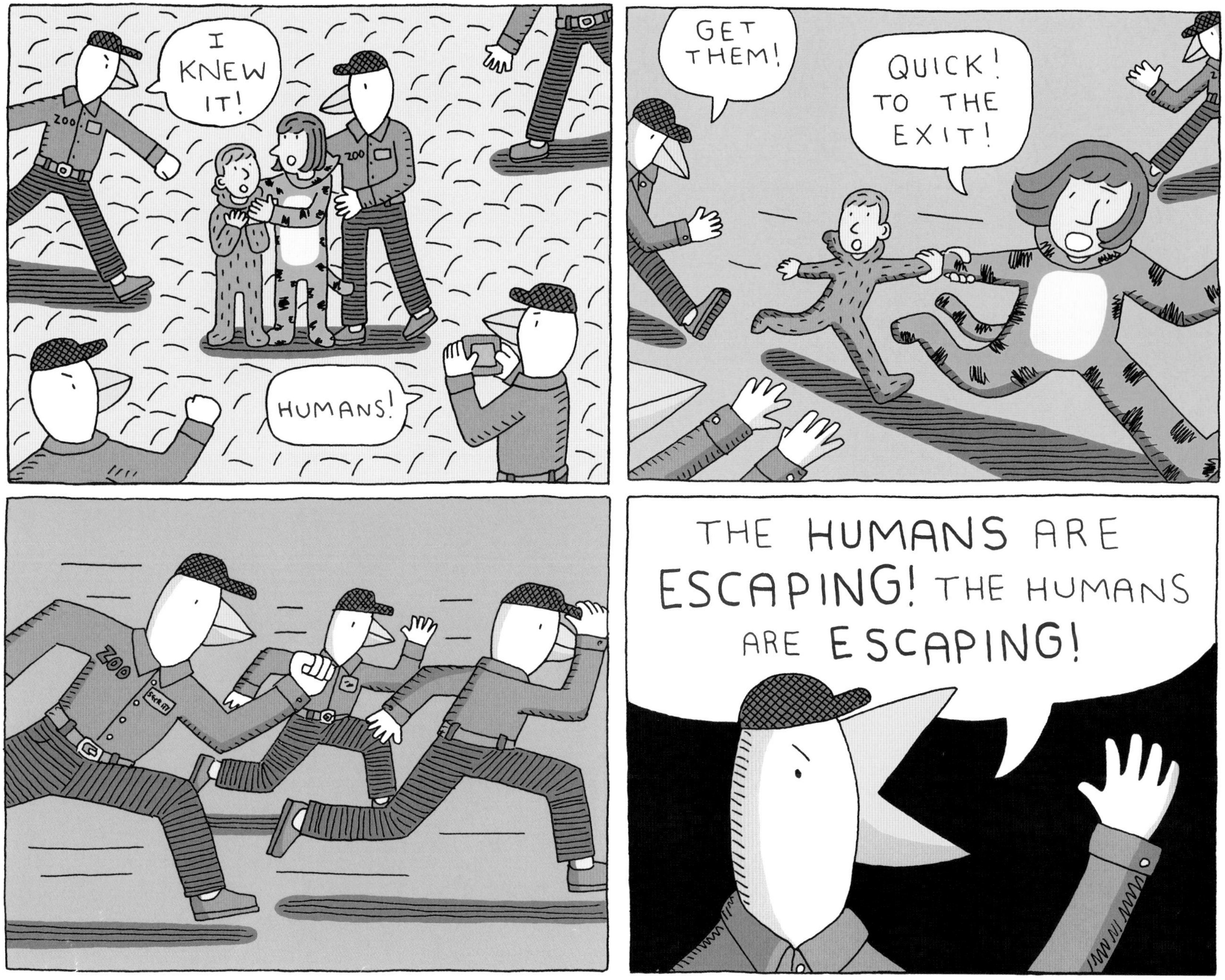
I KNEW IT!
HUMANS!
GET THEM!
QUICK! TO THE EXIT!
THE HUMANS ARE ESCAPING! THE HUMANS ARE ESCAPING!

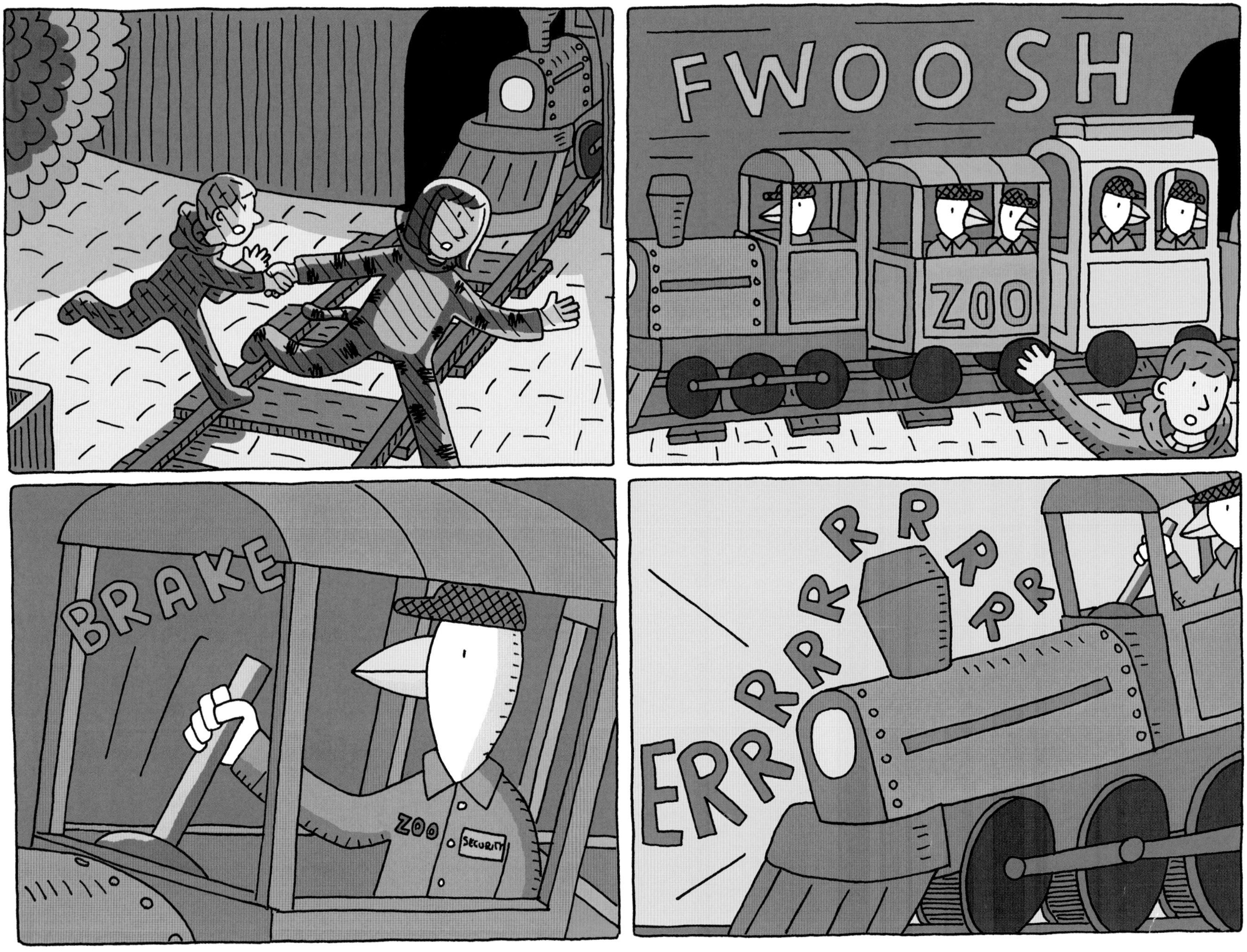
FWOOSH
ZOO
BRAKE
ZOO
SECURITY
ERRRRRRRRRR

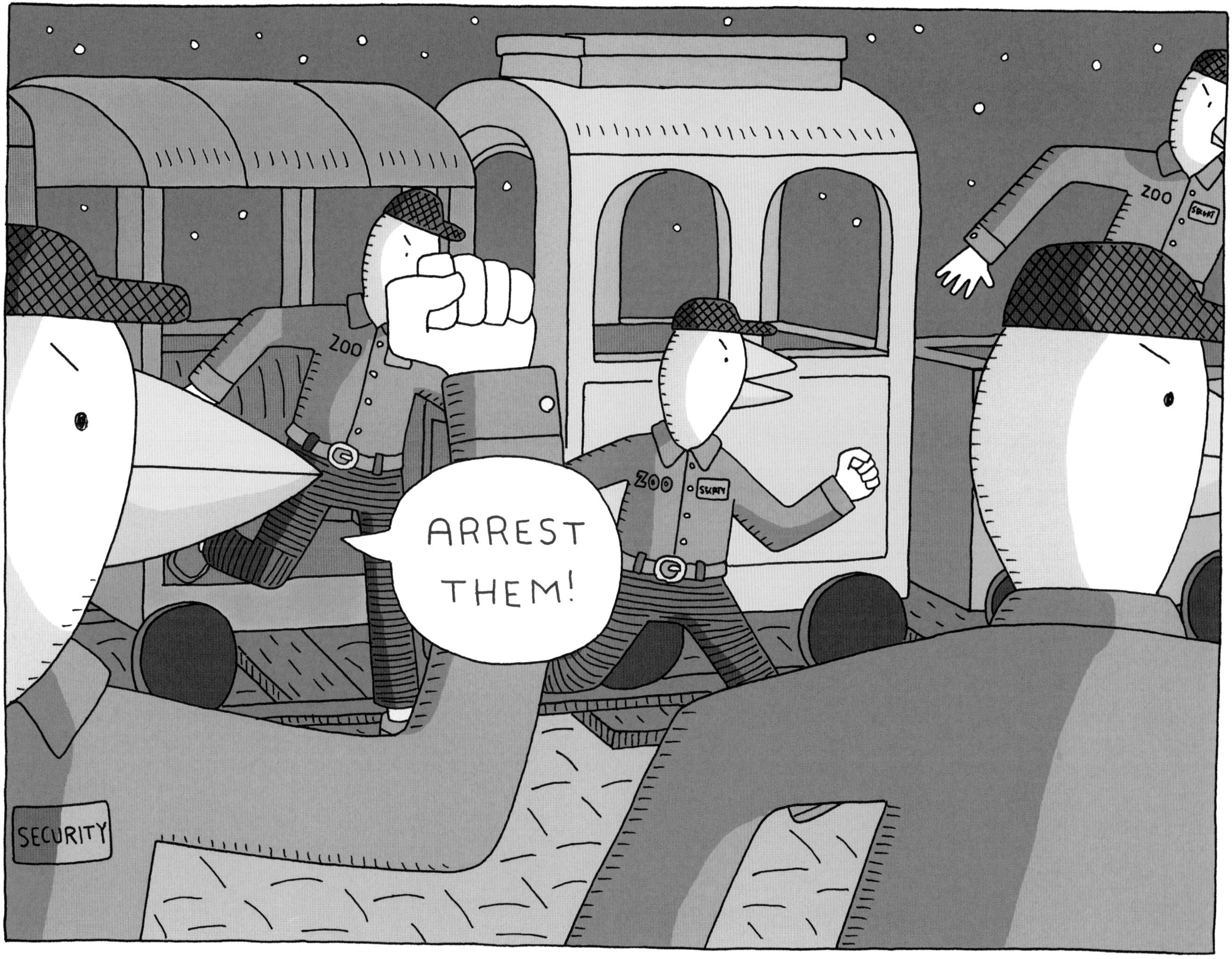
ZOO
ZOO
SECURITY
ARREST THEM!
ZOO
SECURITY

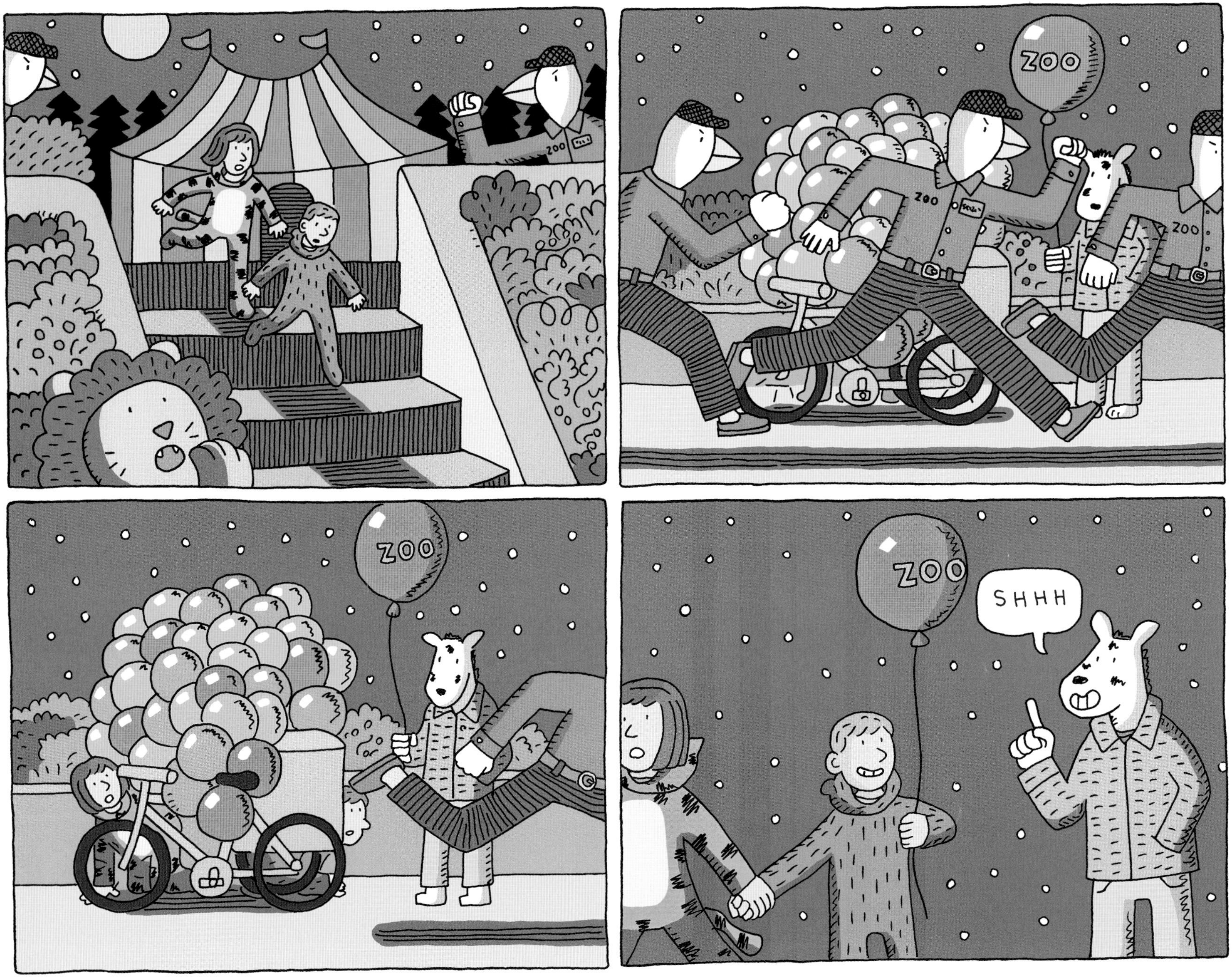
ZOO
ZOO
ZOO
ZOO
ZOO
ZOO
SHHH

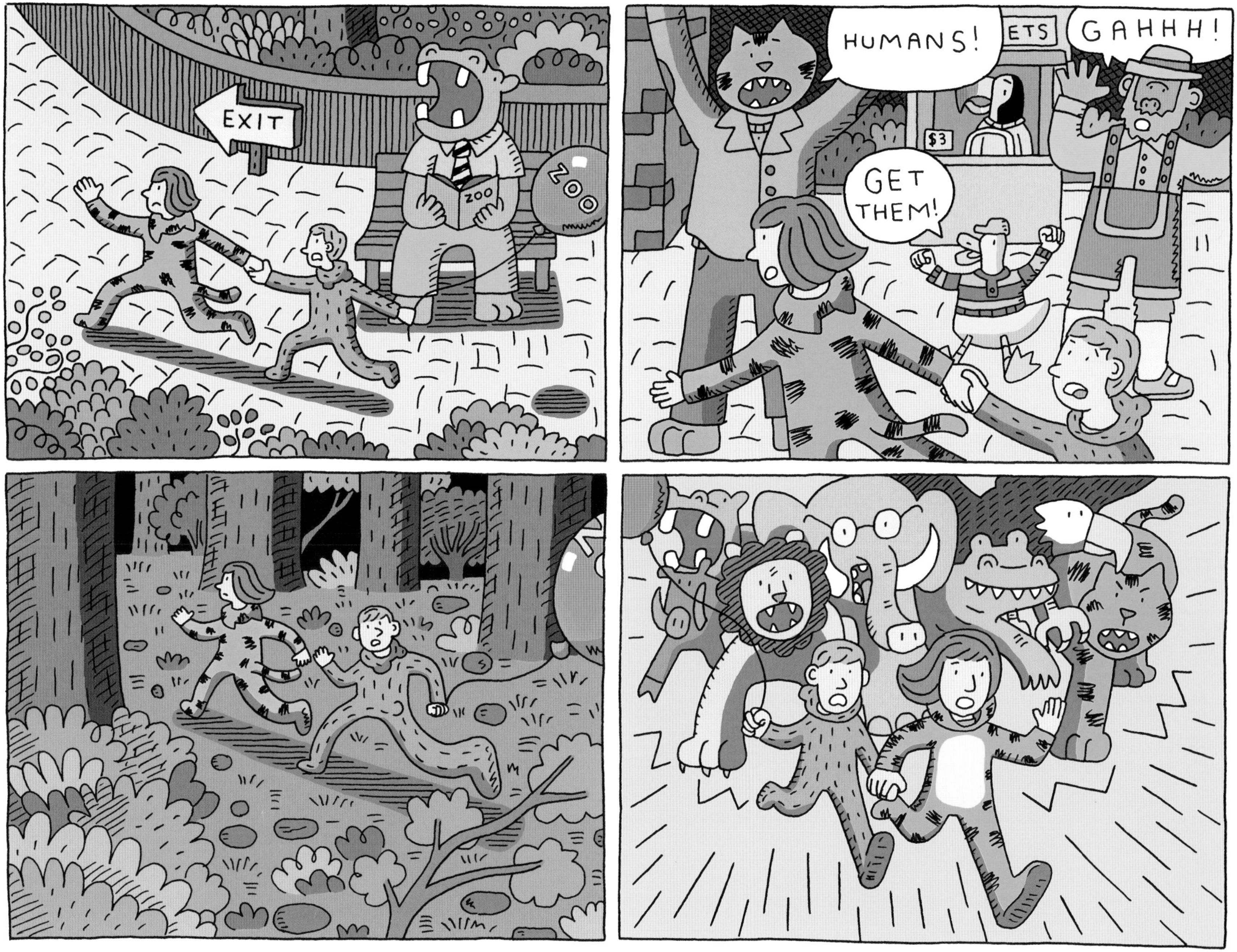
EXIT
ZOO
ZOO
HUMANS!
ETS
GAHHH!
$3
GET THEM!

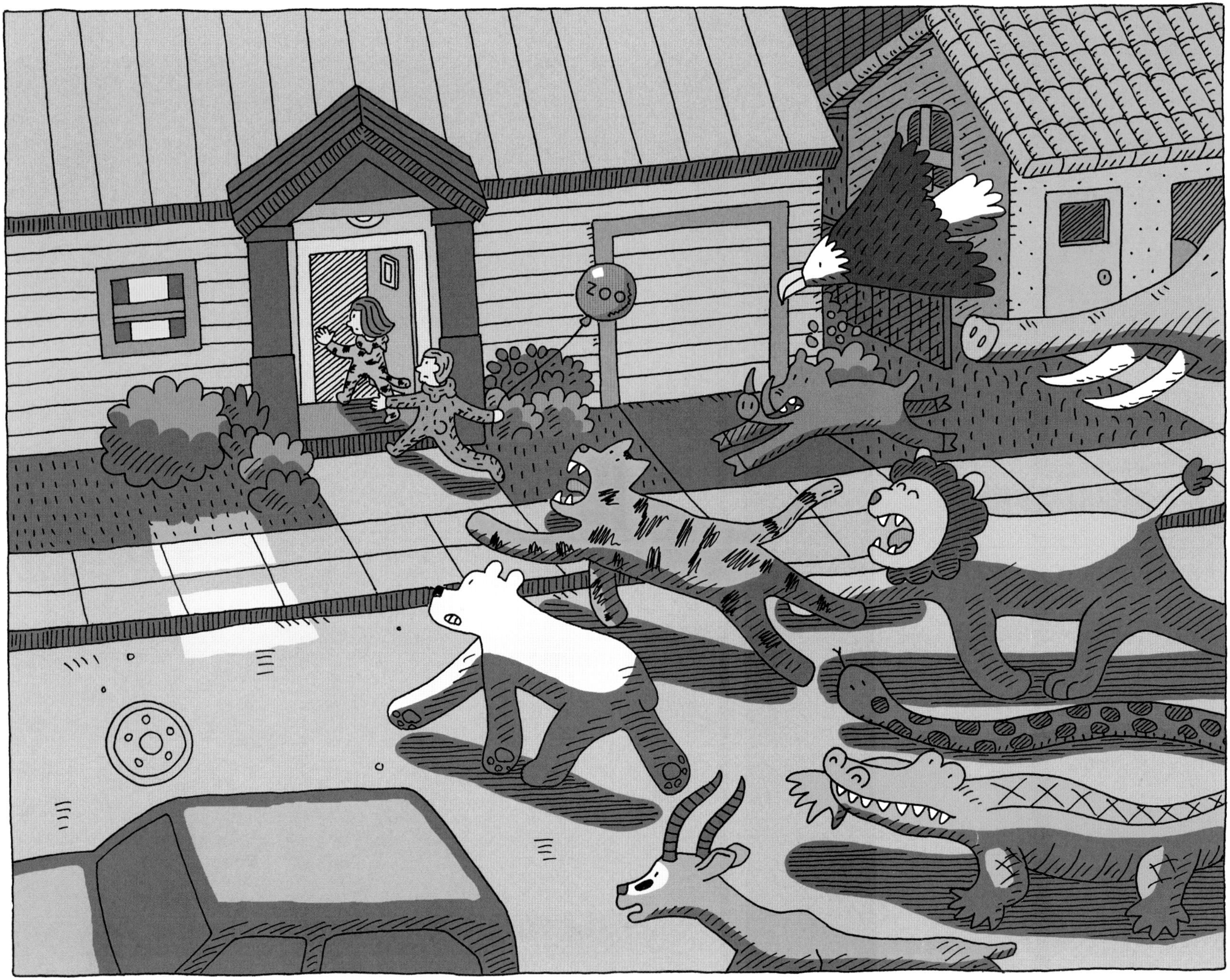
ZOO

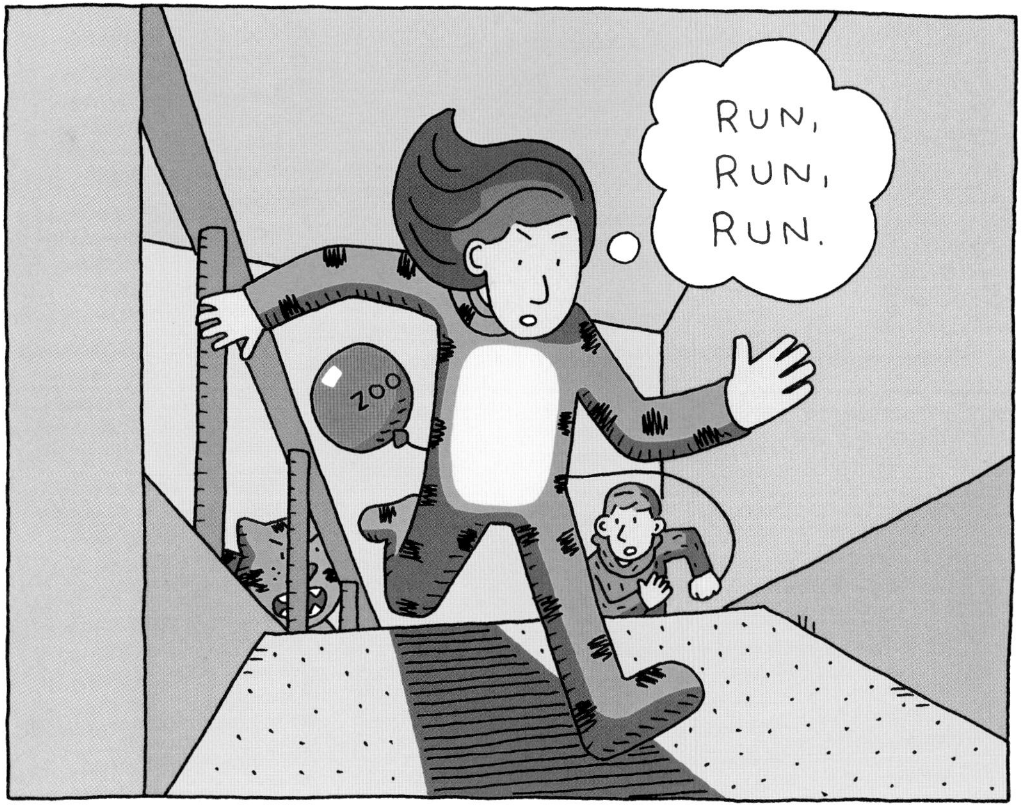
ZOO
RUN,
RUN,
RUN.

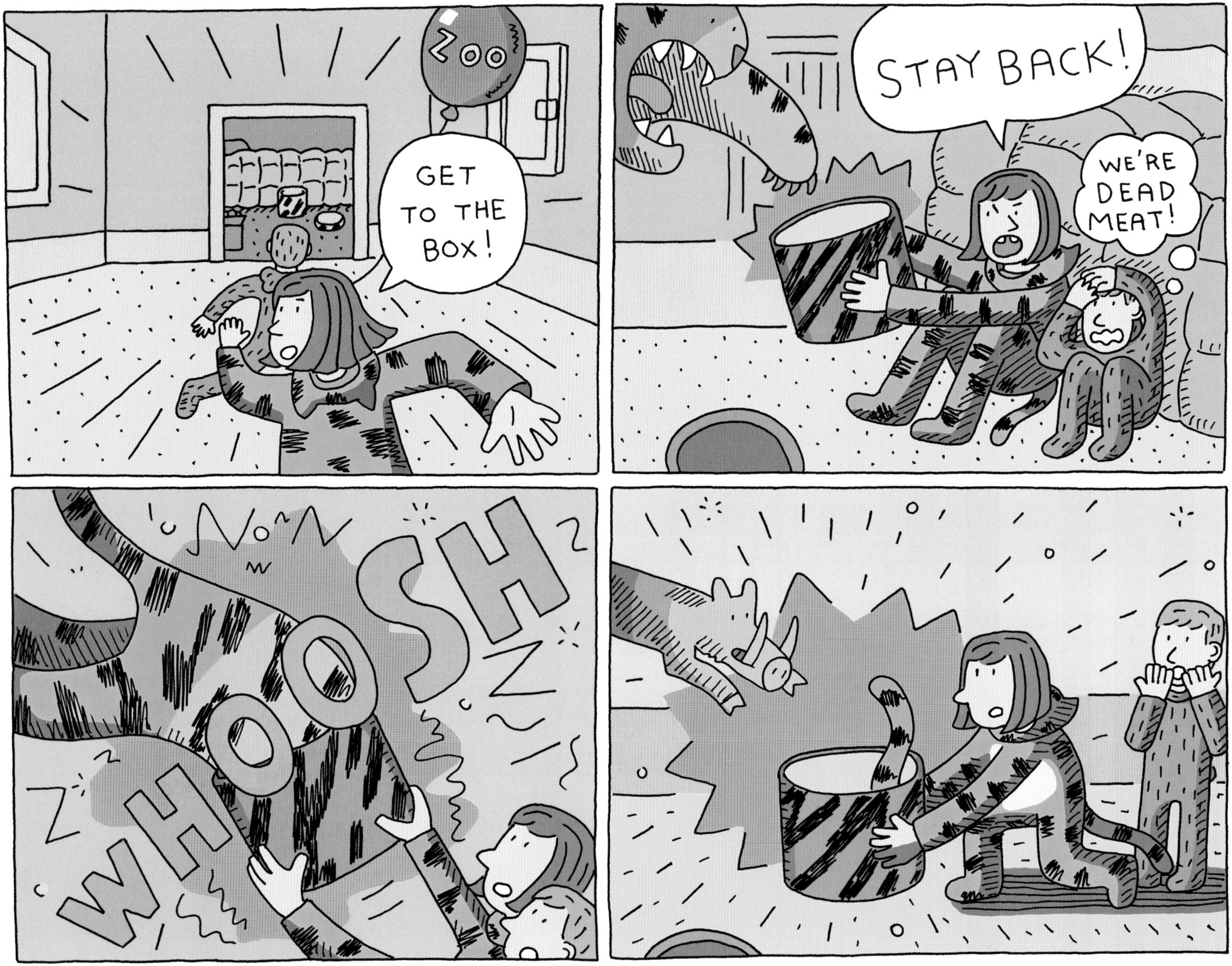
ZOO
GET TO THE BOX!
STAY BACK!
WE'RE DEAD MEAT!
WHOOSH

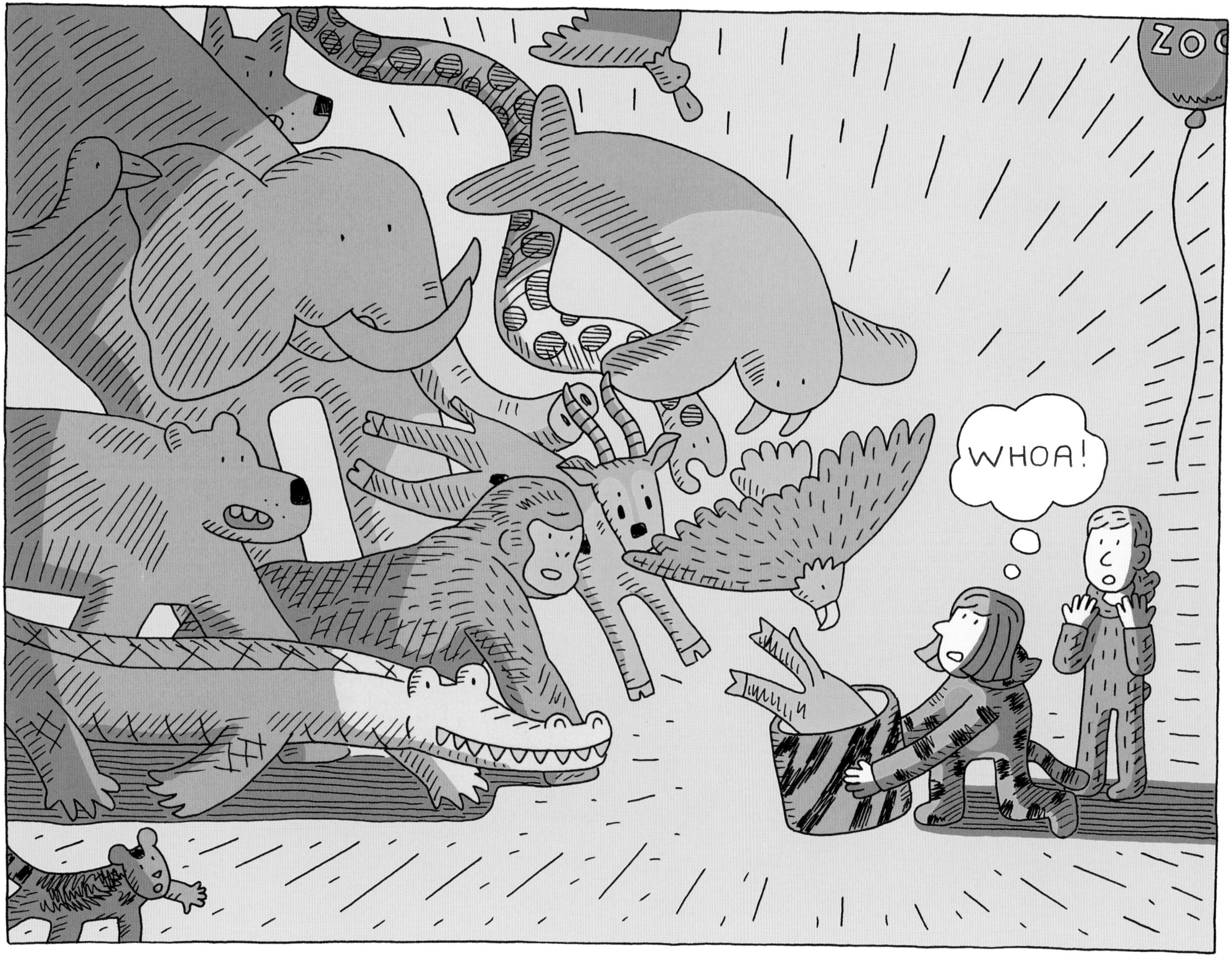
ZOO
WHOA!

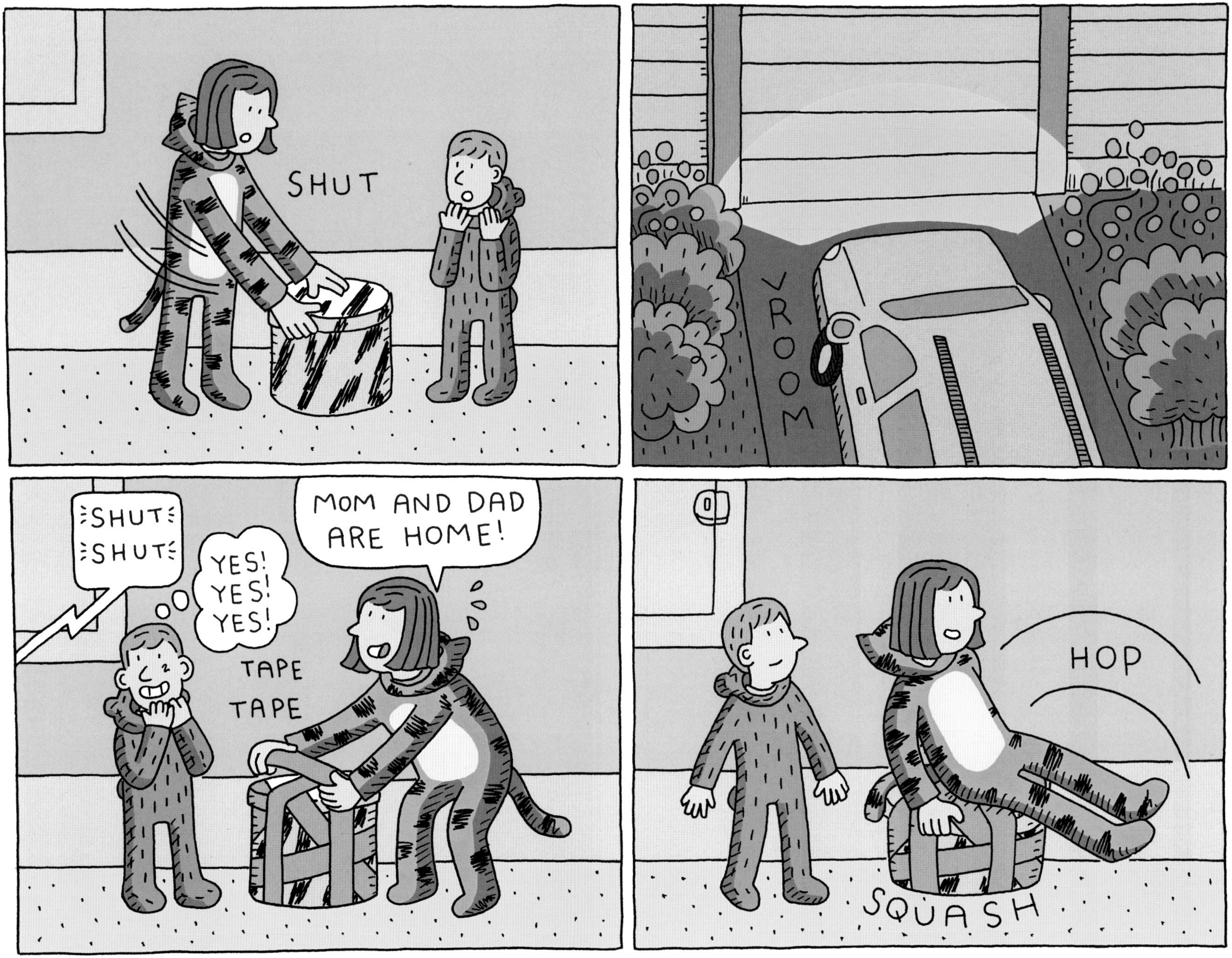
SHUT
VROOM
SHUT SHUT
YES! YES! YES!
MOM AND DAD ARE HOME!
TAPE
TAPE
HOP
SQUASH

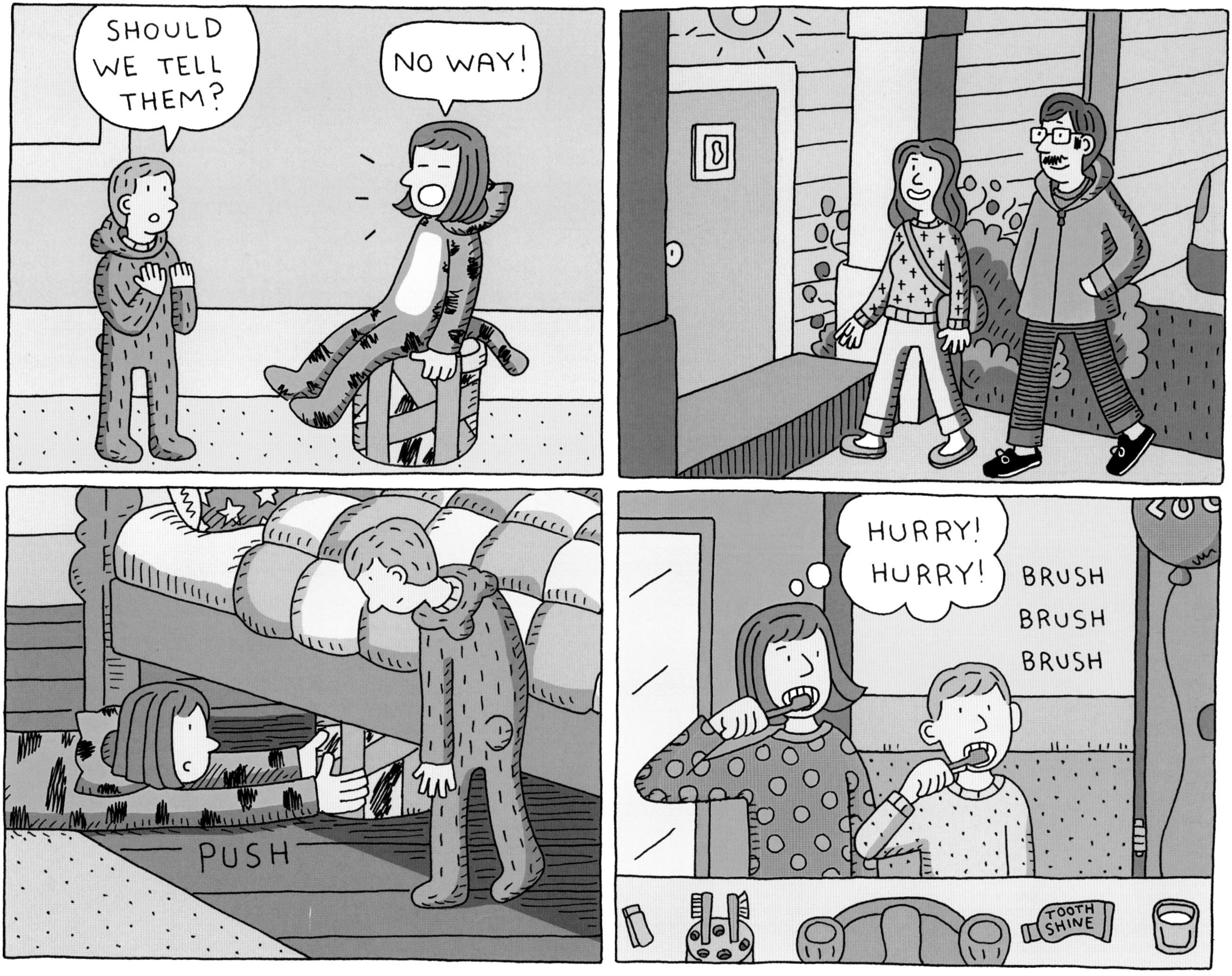
SHOULD WE TELL THEM?
NO WAY!
PUSH
HURRY! HURRY!
BRUSH BRUSH BRUSH
TOOTH SHINE

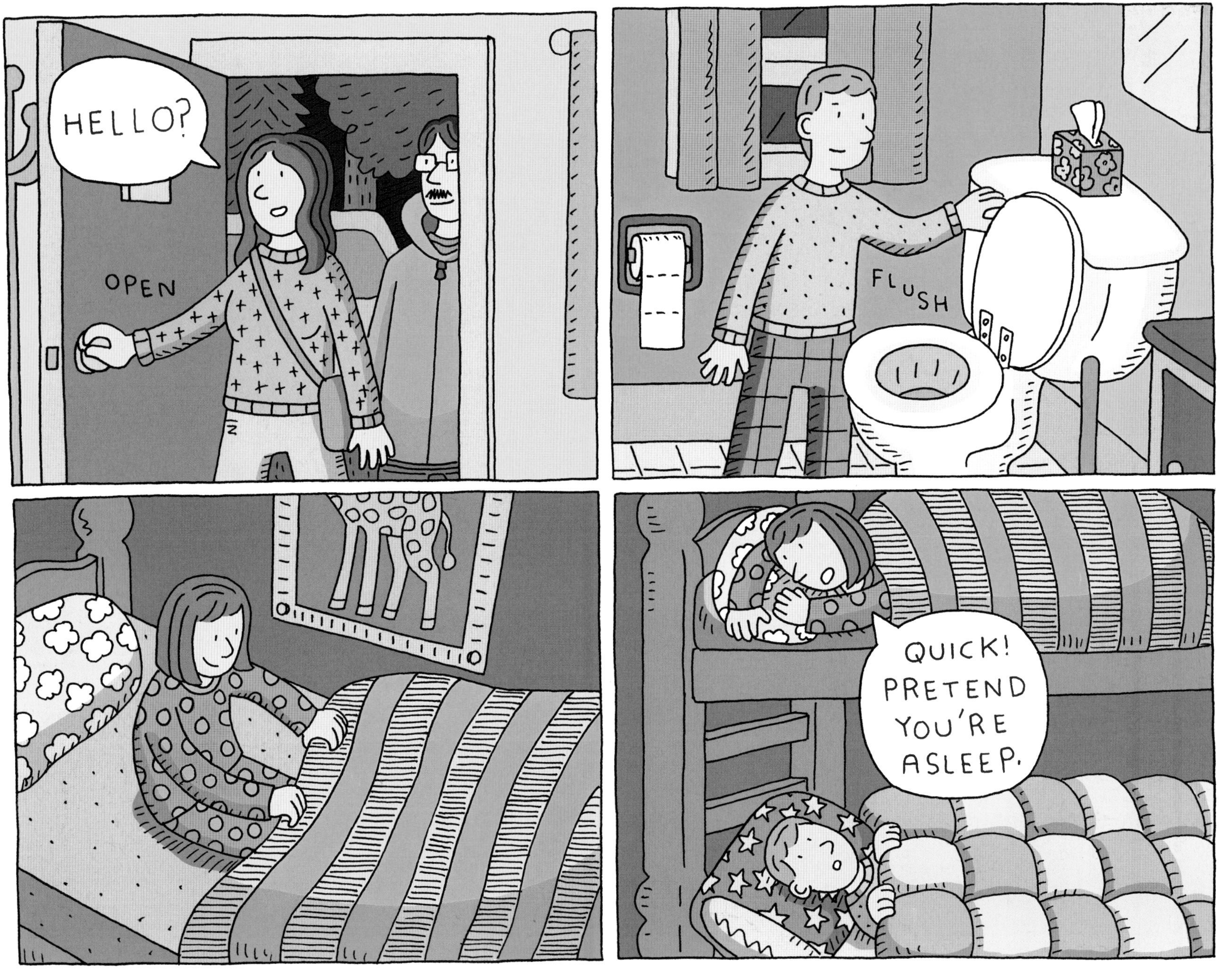
HELLO?
OPEN
FLUSH
QUICK! PRETEND YOU'RE ASLEEP.

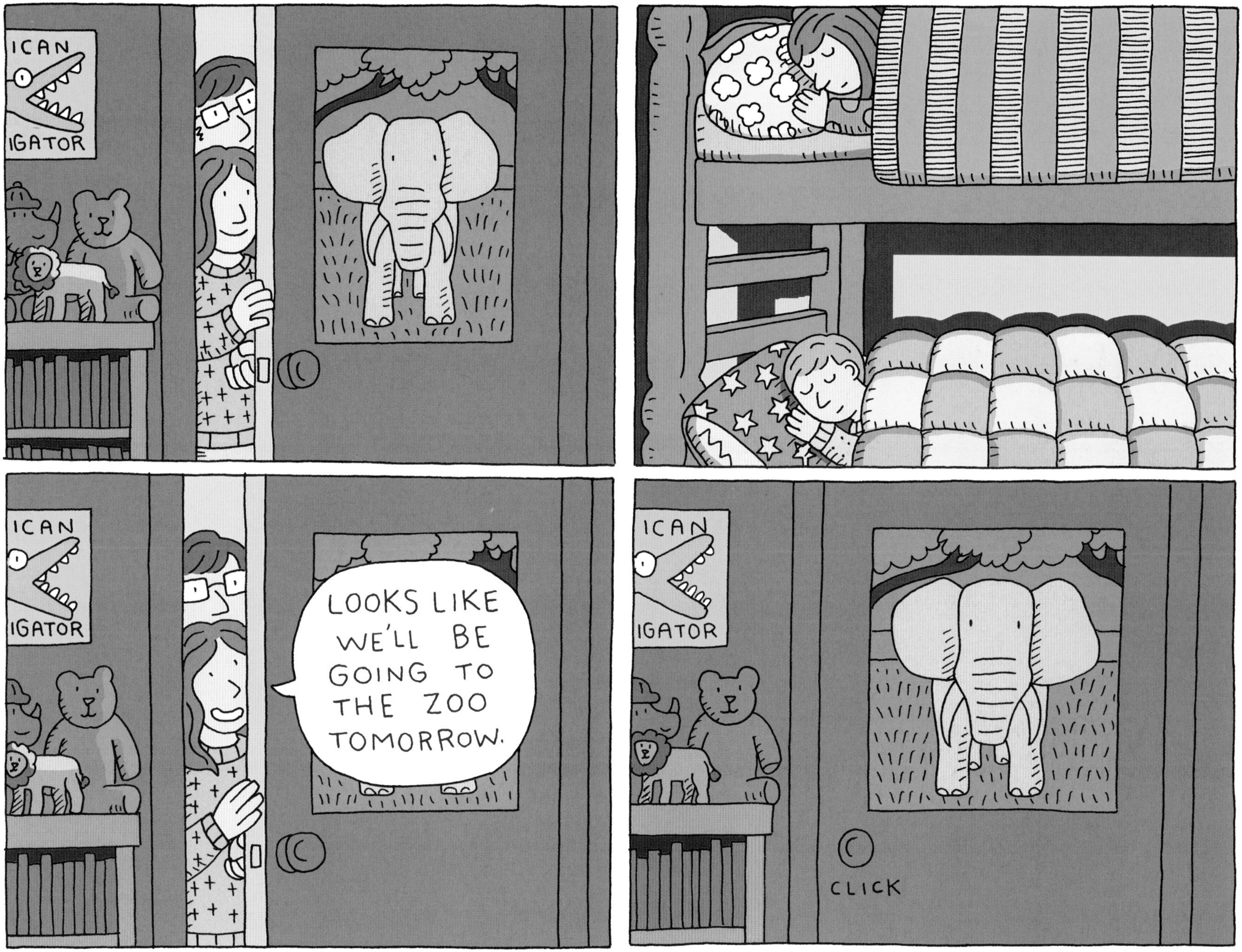
ICAN
IGATOR
ICAN
IGATOR
LOOKS LIKE WE'LL BE GOING TO THE ZOO TOMORROW.
ICAN
IGATOR
CLICK

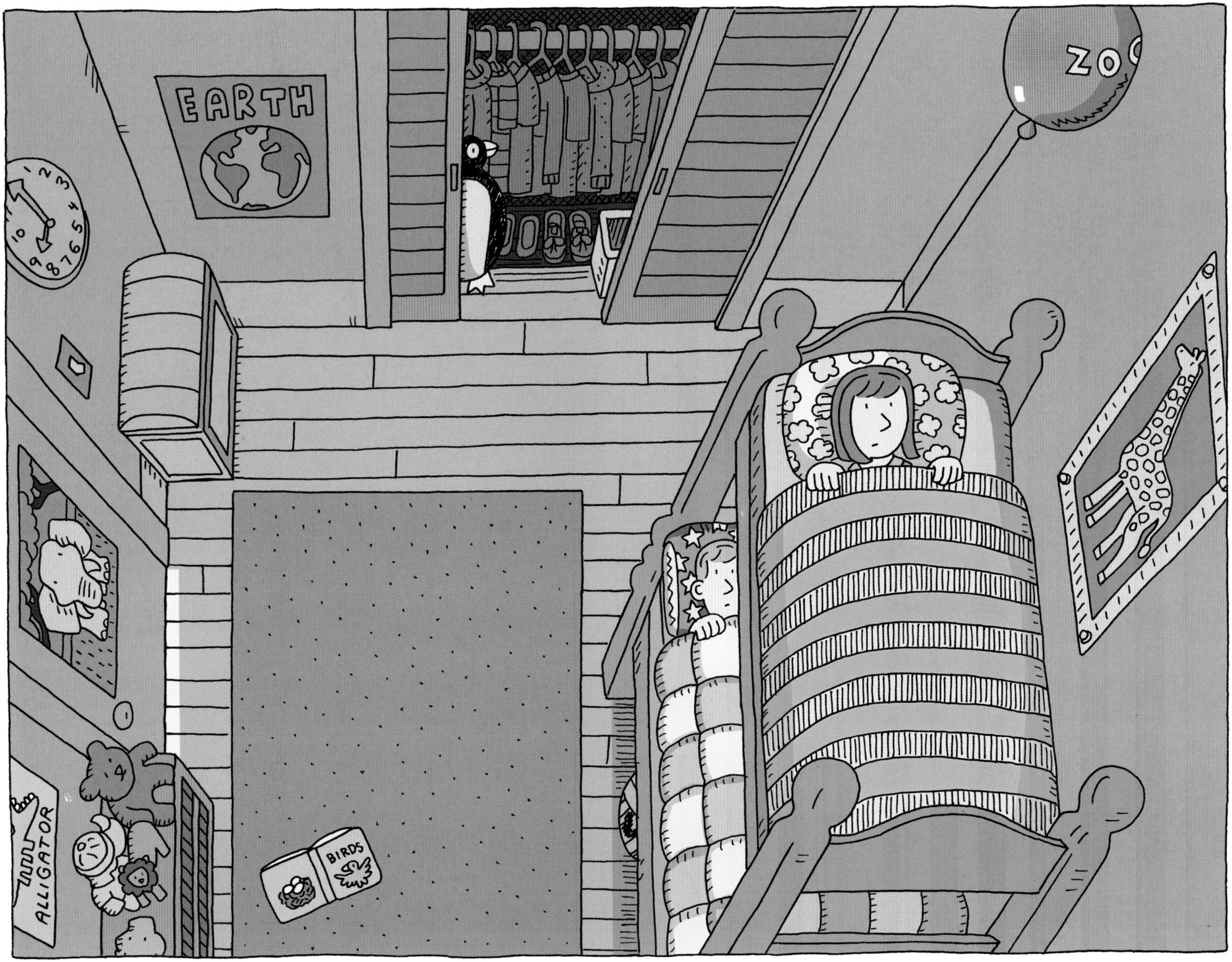
EARTH
ZO
BIRDS
ALLIGATOR